Sherlock Holmes
and the
Frightened Chambermaid

John Hall

Breese Books

THE Publisher for Quality Murder Mystery Books &
Home to the Breese Books Sherlock Holmes Collection

First published in 2023 by
Baker Street Studios Ltd for
Breese Books
Endeavour House
170 Woodland Road, Sawston
Cambridge, CB22 3DX, UK

ISBN: 978-1-901091-84-7 (13 digit)

Front Cover Illustration: The Bank of England in 1896,
as featured in *Round London*.
Back Cover Illustration: The Bank of England's Printing Room in 1854,
as featured in *The Illustrated News*.

Typeset in 8/11/20pt Palatino

The courtyard of the Bank of England in 1903,
As featured in *Living London*.

One

Mr. Sherlock Holmes, who that morning had risen somewhat later than was his custom, put down his coffee cup, lit his pipe, and gazed at me reflectively. "Planning a holiday, Watson?" he asked.

"Your powers of observation and deduction are truly remarkable, Holmes," I said, looking round ruefully at the great mound of leaflets which I had received from various inns, hostelries and hotels. "It is no easy task to wade through all these prospectuses. Or should that be *prospecti,* I wonder?"

Holmes ignored the classical point of grammar. "But you have settled on one at last, though? I deduce that from the great sigh of relief which you emitted a moment ago."

"Yes, this will, I fancy, be my choice, Holmes. The Bell Hotel. 'Set among woodland and meadow, within a stone's throw of the sea, The Bell guarantees the weary guest a restful stay, free from the cares of the workaday world. N.B. sporting gentlemen are advised that excellent shooting and fishing may be had locally, at reasonable rates, by the day or the week'." And I threw the prospectus down, and asked, "What say you to that, Holmes?"

Holmes nodded. "It sounds ideal." He riffled through the post which had arrived not long before. "Nothing out of the ordinary here, Watson." He gazed at me. "You know, Doctor, I have half a mind to join you, for I have been working rather hard just lately."

"I should be delighted if you could spare the time!" said I. "But will you not be taking yourself away from your work?" He waved a hand at the post on the table before him. "I have concluded my most recent cases, and, as I say, there is little offered to me at the moment which promises to be of interest. Yes, I think I shall join you. It promises to be a delightful place."

"And we shall have a complete respite from detection and mystery, murder and mayhem, and all the troubles of the world."

Holmes was right, as always, it was a delightful place. But I, as you shall see, could not have been more wrong.

*****

As it turned out, Holmes was obliged to put some finishing touches to one of his cases, with the result that we did not arrive at The Bell Hotel until late in the evening. It was July, and the sun was low in the sky, but had not yet set, and was painting the great canvas of the heavens with golds and reds.

The hotel, too – this was years go, you must bear in mind, and the place was by no means the same as it is today – was lit up by the sun, all the windows ablaze. I was ready for my dinner, though, and so we did not linger to admire the view. By the time we had dined it was dark, and the journey had been a tiring one, so we lost little time in finding our rooms and retiring.

I woke early next morning, and determined to make amends for missing the views on the previous evening by taking a long walk, which would also sharpen my appetite for breakfast. I listened at Holmes's door – for we had adjoining rooms, and a comfortable sitting room shared between us – as long as I politely could, but heard nothing. Holmes, when he has no detective work in hand, is a sound sleeper, and I did not wish to disturb him. I made my way downstairs alone, then, and headed for the front door. The hall porter seemed surprised to see one of his guests up and about so early, but greeted me cheerfully. "Going out for a walk," I told him. "Can you recommend anywhere in particular for the views?"

6

"Most of them go along the woodland path, sir, and to the cliffs. A fine view for artists and what have you, but a goodish walk, mind you, if you want to be back for breakfast."

"Ah, yes, breakfast, to be sure. Perhaps a shorter route?"

"Yes, sir. Round the meadow, up the little hill, gives you a sight of the cathedral five miles off. Back in half an hour, sir. Thank you, sir."

I started for the door, then remembered something. I muttered a mild reproof at myself, and turned back. "Forgotten something, sir?" asked the porter.

"Yes, my stick. Forget my own head if it wasn't screwed on, these days! Back in a jiffy."

"No need, sir," he assured me. He reached behind the desk, and produced a nice old ash plant. "I keep a stick or two, and a couple of umbrellas, for precisely this eventuality, sir. Just you leave it here when you get back, if you'd be so kind."

I thanked him, and went out. I took the way the porter had indicated, and soon found the little wooded hill. I spent a few minutes there, gazing at the old cathedral city just visible through the early morning mists, and then, ready for an excellent breakfast, I set off back.

It was still early when I reached the hotel, and few guests were up and about. Holmes was nowhere to be seen downstairs, and I set off up to our rooms to rouse him from his slumbers. As I reached the top of the steps that led to our landing, I realized that I still had the stick which the porter had so generously loaned me. I turned, and started back down the stairs. As I did so, I almost bumped into an attractive young woman dressed in the conventional uniform of a chambermaid. I hastily stepped back, mumbling apologies.

I have said that the chambermaid was attractive; to be more accurate, I should have said rather that she would have been attractive, with her jet black hair, pert little face, and bright eyes – but there was upon her face a look as of mortal terror. "What is it, child?" I asked at once, all my chivalrous instincts to the fore. "What has frightened you like this?"

The little chambermaid did not reply, but bustled up the last few stairs to the landing, and ran off down the corridor. I stood there a moment, indecisive, then, feeling that I could and should have done more to assist her to resolve whatever problem so perturbed her, I set off after her. At the end of the corridor I turned the way she had gone, and came to a halt. The corridor now divided after a few yards, and I could not well say whether the maid had taken the left-hand passage or the right. I glanced down both, but they were both deserted. The only sign that anyone had been there was a little gold bracelet, right at my feet, but too far from the place where the corridors diverged to indicate any direction.

Feeling rather puzzled, I picked the bracelet up and returned to our sitting room, to find that Holmes had risen. He was smoking his old briar pipe and staring out of the window. He looked up as I entered. "You look perturbed, Watson."

"Curious thing just now, Holmes. I've just seen one of the maids, and she looked positively terrified."

Holmes raised an eyebrow. "Your much vaunted usual expertise has let you down, then?"

"This is a serious matter, Holmes! The poor young woman had a look of mortal terror on her face."

He swivelled round to look at me properly. "You are upset, Watson, that much is clear. And your concern for this girl's welfare does you credit. Forgive my misplaced attempt at levity. Did you enquire of her as to what had caused this – this mortal terror which you describe?"

"I never got the chance. The maid simply ran off, in the most literal sense, and by the time I had recovered my scattered wits and set off after her, she was out of sight."

"H'mm. That is curious."

"And nothing more? It does not move you to investigate further?"

Holmes yawned. "You forget I am here for a rest, Watson," he told me, a note of complaint in his voice. "Look here, you know my methods. Will you not apply them to a strictly hypothetical study of the problem you have outlined?"

8

"Work out why the maid was scared, you mean?" I sat down. "Very well, Holmes! You sit there, and I'll try my ideas out on you."

Holmes laughed, but he took the seat I had indicated, and refilled his pipe. "Proceed, Doctor."

"The young lady was not merely embarrassed, as she might have been had she walked in upon one of the gentlemen guests having a wash or a shave in his nightgown; and besides, she would, in a sense, be inured to that sort of thing. And then few guests are about, for the wildfowlers have turned out hours ago, and the fishermen are still abed."

Holmes nodded. "But perhaps there were more sinister aspects? One hesitates to suggest the possibility, but some guest may perhaps have forgotten to behave like a gentleman?"

"Holmes!"

"You entirely dismiss the possibility, then?"

"Say rather that I find it a distasteful one. And in any case, would the maid not hasten to report such an occurrence to the manager? It seemed to me from our short acquaintance that he would not tolerate any untoward behaviour in his hotel."

"H'mm. Perhaps, though, the girl was on her way to see the manager when she bumped into you? Shaken by the earlier occurrence, she may have misunderstood your motives?"

I shook my head. "Unlikely, to be blunt, Holmes. Far more likely that she should cry out to me to assist her."

"Well, then, could it not be that something occurred to upset, to frighten, the poor lass before ever she started her duties in the hotel? Perhaps she lives in the village, and something unpleasant happened as she was walking to work?"

"Chambermaids live in, as a rule," I reminded him. "Whatever it was, it must have happened here, in the hotel, and shortly before I bumped into her."

"Ah, you bumped into her?"

"All but. I had just set off down the stairs, and she was coming up them. I was startled myself, so she too must have been taken by surprise, as it were, but that would hardly account for the look of sheer terror. And now that I think about it, she cannot have been going to see the manager, for if she were then she would be going downstairs and not up. A bit of a puzzle, Holmes."

"H'mm," said Holmes yet again. "Well, but it seems to me that there is only one way to resolve the question."

"And what might that be?"

"Send for the maid and ask her!"

This struck me as eminently sensible advice, and I immediately rang the bell. A couple of minutes later there came a tap at the door. "Come in!" I called.

The door opened, and a tall young woman with long blonde hair stood there. "You rang, sir?"

"Ah, yes." I stood there, embarrassed. After all, I could hardly tell this maid that I wanted another girl altogether, now could I? It would be misunderstood, no doubt of that. Indeed, Holmes and I might very well be told to leave the hotel! And then I remembered the little gold bracelet that I had found. I took it out and held it up. "It was one of your colleagues that I really wished to have a word with. Small, attractive, with very dark hair. She was here earlier, in the corridor outside, that is to say, and must have dropped this. I merely wished to return it to her."

The maid glanced at the bracelet, and shook her head. "I don't think it would belong to any of the maids here, sir," she told me doubtfully.

"And why not?"

"Well, sir, for one thing it's too valuable. A chambermaid might own such a thing, but she wouldn't wear it to work."

Holmes put in, "I see. You said, 'For one thing', though?"

The maid frowned. "Well, sir, I don't think it can have been one of the maids, because there isn't a maid such as you mentioned working here."

"On this floor, you mean?"

"In the whole hotel, sir. The manager would tell you the very same thing, I'm sure."

"Oh." I stood there, not quite knowing what to say next.

Holmes said, in his most careless tone, "You are right, of course. Watson here must have been mistaken, and this must belong to one of the guests. We shall see the manager and return it to him, for its owner will probably ask him about it. Thank you," and he handed the maid a shilling.

When she had gone, I turned to Holmes in some mild exasperation. "Must have been mistaken, indeed! I assure you ..."

"And I assure you, Watson, that insisting upon what you had seen would merely have caused a good deal of unhelpful gossip. This way, the matter will be forgotten quickly, at least by those whom it does not concern, and we shall be able to investigate it more easily."

"Ahah!" I was mollified, but in no mood to let him off that easily. "And I thought you wanted a rest cure?"

Holmes laughed in his singular silent fashion. "A change of work is the best rest, Watson." He stood up. "I propose that we delay our breakfast, and see the manager ... "

"And I propose that we don't! The matter is hardly so important that we should miss sampling The Bell's celebrated cuisine, Holmes."

"Perhaps you are right," he replied, with some reluctance.

I led the way downstairs, and into the dining room, where we did indeed find that the hotel's claims as to its food were justified. Holmes, as was his way when he was thinking over a problem, was at first inclined to do no more than play with what was on his plate, but when I reminded him that – according to him – I might very well have been mistaken about the whole episode, he laughed, and then made as hearty a breakfast as I did myself.

When we had finished, Holmes stood up. "Perhaps now would be as good a time as any to see the manager," he said, and set off for the reception desk.

"Anything the matter, Mr. Holmes?" asked the manager anxiously, when he emerged from his office.

"No, no. Far from it. It was merely that Dr. Watson here has found a lady's bracelet, and, since we do not know to whom it might belong, we wished to hand it over to you. I had a notion it was dropped by one of the maids – smallish, jet black hair, pretty?"

The manager shook his head. "None of the maids answers that description, Mr. Holmes. However, it does sound like one of the guests, a Miss Dennison."

"Ah!" Holmes glanced casually back at the door to the dining room. "And is Miss Dennison down to breakfast, would you know?"

"I have been in my office, I fear." The manager crossed to the reception desk, and asked the receptionist, "Has Miss Dennison been down, do you know?"

"I have not seen her, sir. But her father came down to breakfast not five minutes ago, and must still be in the dining room."

"Thank you." The manager raised an eyebrow at Holmes. "I could return the bracelet to Mr. Dennison, if you wish?"

"Please do not trouble yourself," said Holmes. "We have no plans for the day, and can easily spare five minutes. What does Mr. Dennison look like, by the way?" he asked as he made for the door which led to the dining room.

"Oh, thick-set, a fine head of hair, almost completely grey, heavy moustache, tweeds. He and his daughter are probably at one of the little tables for two by the window."

Holmes nodded. "Thank you. You may rely upon us to return the bracelet."

The manager smiled, and returned to his duties in his office. Holmes pushed the door open, and glanced round the dining room. There was but one man who answered the manager's description, and he sat, alone, by the window at one of the tables mentioned. I had not seen him before – as I said, we had arrived somewhat late the previous evening, and so had no opportunity to meet many of our fellow guests.

Holmes walked up to the table. "Mr. Dennison?"

He looked up, a frown upon his face. "Yes, I am Charles Dennison. What can I do for you, sir?"

"It is more a question of what we may be able to do for you," said Holmes. "I am Sherlock Holmes, and this is Dr. John Watson."

I was studying Dennison closely, and at the mention of Holmes's name I saw a curious look flash over Dennison's face. It is, of course, not an unusual thing for the name of Sherlock Holmes to produce recognition, for over the years Holmes's fame has spread far and wide. But I could swear that there was something more than mere recognition there. Almost I could have said – fear.

However, Dennison spoke readily enough, and steadily enough. "I have heard of your exploits, of course, gentlemen. Who has not? But I confess that I do not quite see what you mean by your suggestion that you might be helping me?"

Holmes smiled. "It was no very serious matter, sir. Merely that my colleague Dr. Watson here found a little bracelet in the corridor, and we thought it might belong to your daughter."

I produced the bracelet again, and handed it to Dennison, who studied it for a moment. "Yes," he told me, "it belongs to Amy ... my daughter, that is to say. I am obliged to you, sir, and I'm sure Amy will also be most grateful. With your permission I shall keep this and return it to her when next I see her."

Holmes gave the most careless and casual of glances around the room. "Miss Dennison is not down to breakfast yet?"

"My daughter left the hotel late last night."

"Oh?"

Dennison looked down at his plate, as if to indicate delicately that he wished to get on with his breakfast. But Holmes simply stood there, and after a moment Dennison continued, "Amy had a telegram yesterday evening. An old school friend ... a sudden illness ... Amy felt obliged to return, to see what she could do, if anything. I wanted to go with her, but she insisted that I remain until the end of the week, as we had originally intended. Amy is a good girl, but can be a touch assertive, particularly when it comes to her old father." He smiled at us.

"And you had no worries as to letting her travel alone?" asked Holmes.

13

"Oh, no. Perfectly safe, these days. A cab, then a 'Ladies Only' compartment on the train. Perfectly safe." Dennison transferred his gaze to me. "Once again, Doctor, I am much obliged to you for returning my daughter's jewellery."

This time there could be no mistaking his meaning, and I mumbled something appropriate and set off for the door, Holmes following rather reluctantly at my heels. "What do you think to that?" I asked, when we safely out of Dennison's hearing.

"It is a puzzle, is it not?" said Holmes. "If Miss Dennison really did leave the hotel last night, then you could hardly have seen her this morning." He frowned. "And in any event, if she were a paying guest, why on earth should she dress up as a chambermaid?"

"Ah." I too had been thinking about this last aspect of the mystery. "I wondered if perhaps this Dennison were not actually her father?"

Holmes's frown deepened. "I could see that there might be some deception along those lines, indeed the same thought had occurred to me, particularly when Dennison's expression changed as he heard my name. But I still cannot see why the girl should dress up in a maid's uniform."

I sighed. Holmes can be almost unbelievably unworldly at times. Still, it was not for me to enlighten him. I said, "I merely put forward the observation that they may not be related. If so, that might explain the whole thing."

Holmes was about to make some reply, when there came a sudden loud scream from the floor above. Holmes glanced at me, then raced up the stairs. I followed close behind, and as we turned into the corridor that led off the first-floor landing, I saw the maid – the blonde woman who had answered the bell earlier – standing outside one of the rooms, a handkerchief to her face, and sobbing and screaming alternately. A few of the other guests had heard the noise, and stood curiously at their own room doors, wondering what was going on – as, indeed, I was myself.

Holmes pushed the maid aside, more roughly than I thought was necessary, and dived into the room. I paused, to try to comfort the maid, who was clearly most distressed by something she had seen or heard. Could this 'something', I wondered, be the same thing that had upset the other lady, this Miss Dennison, if such was her name?

Before I could pursue the point, or render much assistance to the maid, Holmes reappeared and dragged me into the room, shutting the door behind us.

"Holmes?"

"Your professional skills are needed, Doctor, and quickly." He waved a hand.

I looked where he pointed. I saw firstly an armchair, in which was slumped the body of a man of some thirty-five years of age, handsome enough when he was alive, but now too obviously dead, judging both by his face and by the knife sticking out of his chest. And secondly, upon a sofa of the variety called a Chesterfield, I saw the inert form of the young lady whom I had seen earlier, Miss Dennison, as I now supposed her to be, still in her chambermaid's uniform, which was now liberally stained with blood.

Two

"The man's dead," I said shortly. "No point wasting time on him, poor devil."

"And the girl?"

"Ah, the girl." I made a hasty examination. "Still alive, Holmes. Unconscious. No wound ... Holmes, there is no sign of any wound!"

"The blood must be his, then? But then if there is no wound on the girl ..."

"Bump on the back of the head," I told him. "It's not serious, but that must have been what knocked her out." I stood up. "I really need my bag, Holmes. I shan't be a moment. Doubtless you can use the time wisely," I added, knowing his horror of investigating the scene of any crime after the police and other well-meaning individuals had tramped all over it.

I went out into the corridor, where folk were still standing, wondering what all the fuss might be about. "Here," I said to one of the men, an alert young chap who looked as if he were used to command, an army man, perhaps, "There's been ... ah, an accident. Could ..."

"Anybody hurt?" he asked.

"No, no, nothing serious. Look could you possibly be good enough to fetch the manager, and ask them downstairs to contact the police ... yes, and if you would also be so kind as to ask a Mr. Dennison to step up here? You'll find him in the dining room, I think."

17

"Very good, sir." He hesitated the merest fraction. "Anything else I can do?"

"Not at the moment," I said, "but if we might call upon you later, if needs be?"

He nodded, and ran off on the errand I had set him. I hastened to my room, found my medical bag, and returned to Holmes.

I found him sitting by the side of the girl, who was starting to come round. "Feeling better?" I asked her.

The only answer was a groan – it was, I suppose, a silly question – so I shooed Holmes out of the way and took a look at my patient. There was no great harm done, apart from the bump on the back of her head, which was clearly causing her some pain. But there were no symptoms of concussion, as I had feared there might be. It would, however, be some time before she was sufficiently strong to answer any of the questions which Holmes was pretty obviously bursting to ask her.

Fortunately, at that point there was a tap at the door, and the manager, looking very anxious, came into the room. "Good Heavens!" was his first reaction, logically enough given the circumstances.

"There has been murder done, and we need your help," said Holmes. "First of all, have you sent for the police?"

"Yes, indeed."

"Then could you clear this corridor? Tell the other guests that there has been an accident, but everything is now being straightened out. Do nothing to alarm them, I beg you."

"Very well."

The manager turned to go, but Holmes stopped him. "And the police will need a list of everyone who is in the hotel, staff as well as guests. And a note of anyone who left since yesterday."

"I understand."

"Oh, and one other thing ... who is, or was, rather, the dead man?"

The manager glanced at the body in the chair, and shuddered. "A Mr. Williams," he told us. "Or so he said."

Holmes nodded. "Thank you."

As the manager opened the door to leave, someone else tapped at it, and burst into the room. It was Dennison, if such was his name, and he was in something of a state. "Miss Blake ... ah, Mr. Holmes! I am not overly surprised to find you here, sir." He glanced at my erstwhile patient. "Is she ..."

"A blow to the head only, sir," I told him. "She will be fine in a day or two."

"More to the purpose," said Holmes grimly, "is the question: what exactly is going on here? I take it that this ... Miss Blake, did you say? ... is not your daughter? And I have a sneaking suspicion that Dennison is not your name."

"You are right, Mr. Holmes," said 'Dennison' shortly. "My name is not Dennison, though that will serve for the time being. As to Miss Blake, she is no longer your responsibility, and nor is the investigation into this matter."

"Oh? The local police ..."

"The local police will not be concerned either," said Dennison.

"And how ..."

"They will be instructed that Scotland Yard will take over the case."

Holmes frowned. "I know many of the Yard's officers ..."

"None of whom will be involved, I assure you."

Holmes's frown deepened. "You appear to take much upon yourself, sir."

Dennison sighed. He reached into his pocket, and took out a stiff, thick sheet of paper, which he passed to Holmes. "You will recognize the signature, I'm sure," he said drily.

Holmes glanced at the paper. "Good Lord!"

"Quite so. I shall take over now, Mr. Holmes."

Holmes's attitude had changed markedly when he answered. "If you wish, sir. Only ..."

"Only?"

Holmes waved a hand round the room. "Only you do not appear to have run things very well up to press! Forgive my candour, sir, but Watson and I have some small experience in these matters, as the man who signed your warrant will testify. We are entirely at your disposal, and willing to work under your orders."

Dennison's face clouded, and he strode to the window, where he gazed out, muttering softly to himself. Then he turned, and smiled. "Well, Mr. Holmes, since my superior is your brother, I suppose I can trust you, and the good Doctor here. And I could certainly use some help."

"Mycroft?" I asked. When Holmes nodded, I went on, "Then this matter must involve the government?"

"It does," said Dennison. "And it is of the gravest importance."

"And Miss Blake?" asked Holmes.

"One of my … our … most reliable agents. But young, and thus inexperienced." He scowled, but not at us. "I blame myself for this. I should never have asked her …"

"And where does this dead man, Williams, fit in?" Holmes interrupted.

"He was a suspect. Nay, *the* suspect, for his was the only name we had to work with."

"But of what was he suspected?" I asked from my post at Miss Blake's side. "What the devil is going on?"

"Forgery," said Dennison. He took a five pound note from his pocket, and handed it across to Holmes. "What d'you think to that, Mr. Holmes?"

Now, I have told you that all this happened a long time ago. It was, in fact, a very long time ago, and five pounds then was not what five pounds is today, not by a long chalk. Five pounds was then a decent salary for a week's work in an office in the City, and a sight more than any working man would receive for his week's labours, even with overtime. The five pounds notes of which I write were large, as big as a sheet of writing paper. They were printed on one side only of thick, heavy white paper, and it was not uncommon to find more or less the entire history of the note written on the otherwise blank reverse, for successive owners would jot down little sums, or memoranda of their financial position. The notes, in brief, were imposing, a worthy product of that worthy institution, the Bank of England.

Holmes glanced at it, then studied it more closely, and held it up to the light. "Well, this is a genuine note. Where is your forgery?"

"That is the forgery."

"Nonsense!" Holmes held the note to the light once more. "But … the paper, that is surely genuine. The very watermark!"

"Ah, now you see why we are so concerned?" said Dennison. "These notes have started to appear recently, not in any great quantities as yet, but enough to concern Her Majesty's Treasury." He gave a taut little smile. "As a matter of strict fact, the note is not quite perfect. There is the tiniest of flaws in the printing, so tiny as to be well-nigh imperceptible." He bent over Holmes, touched the note. "There."

"Ah! Well, once it is pointed out, it becomes merely a matter of checking every note one may receive. Why not circulate a note of the flaw …"

"And alert the forgers to their carelessness? Allow them to correct the fault before we catch up with them?" Dennison's tone was heavy with sarcasm.

"H"mm." Holmes thought for a moment. "So the only thing to be done is catch the gang … we must assume it is a gang, the work is so nearly perfect … before too much damage is done?"

Dennison nodded. "You have it, sir. And that is precisely what Miss Blake and I were trying to do, when this happened."

"And the maid's uniform?" I asked. "What was that all about?"

"Oh, Williams had never seen either Miss Blake or myself, so far as we knew," said Dennison. "Miss Blake borrowed the uniform from one of the maids, with some notion of getting a look inside Williams's room."

"It looks as if she succeeded!" I remarked. At that point, Miss Blake struggled to say something. "Do not distress yourself, madam," I told her.

But Holmes put in eagerly, "Nay, she is almost herself again. Tell me, Miss Blake, did you see the man who struck you? The man who killed Williams?"

"No," said Miss Blake. "I came to the room disguised as a maid, just as Mr. Dennison says, hoping to get a look round."

"What time was that?" asked Holmes quickly.

"Oh, when Mr Dennison went to his breakfast." Dennison confirmed this with a nod. Miss Blake went on, "I tapped on the door, and there was no reply. I assumed that Williams had also gone to his breakfast, and that I could take a look round in safety. The real maids do not come to tidy the rooms until breakfast is quite finished, so there was no danger of being disturbed by them. And if Williams came back, I should apologize for disturbing him, and say I would come back later to finish tidying the room."

Holmes nodded approval. "A clever scheme. But I take it that when you opened the door, you saw the body lying on the floor?"

I was about to correct him by saying that the body was in the armchair, then realized that he might be testing Miss Blake. And when she replied, "Yes, that is so," I thought I must be right.

Holmes nodded again. "You did not move the body to the armchair?"

Miss Blake looked surprised. "No. Why do you ask that?"

"It was there, exactly as you see, that we found him. But he had been moved, for there is a spot of blood on the carpet, yonder."

"It was there that I saw him," said Miss Blake, looking at the carpet where Holmes pointed. "I bent over him, to see whether there might still be some glimmer of life, and then …"

"You were struck from behind?"

Miss Blake nodded. "I recall falling forward, on to the body, hence …" and she indicated the blood on her apron, and shuddered.

"Just so," said Holmes in his most soothing tone.

"And then I remembered nothing more until just now."

Puzzled, I asked, "But why move the body? Come to that, having killed a man and left the room ... for I take it Miss Blake's assailant was not hiding in here with the body ... then why return at all?"

"Oh, that is clear," said Holmes. "The murderer wished to search the body. That is why it was moved. Odd that he did not do so immediately after killing him, though? Unless he did search him, thought he had found what he sought, then realized later that something was missing? Yes, that is the most likely explanation, I fancy." He moved to the body, and ran his hands quickly through the pockets. "Hullo!" He took out a large crocodile leather notecase, flipped it open, and whistled. "Whatever was taken, it wasn't money." He held up a thick wad of five pound notes.

"May I?" Dennison checked the notes rapidly. "Fakes," he told us.

"All of them?"

"H'mm. No, not all of them." Dennison looked more closely at the notes. "Sixty pounds in genuine currency, but some two hundred and ten ... no, fifteen pounds in forged notes."

"What on earth was the killer looking for, then?" I wondered. "Assuming that the body was moved in order to search it, of course."

"It must have been," said Holmes, half to himself. "Why else would it be moved?"

Further speculation was cut short by the arrival of the official forces, in the shape of a young police constable from the local station. Dennison produced his letter of authority, and explained matters in a few words. The constable regarded Dennison with considerable awe, Holmes, whose name was well-known, with only slightly less awe, and me, I regret to say, with no awe at all. He was an alert and eager young man, that constable, but this sort of thing was pretty obviously out of his experience. He seemed relieved when Dennison said that we would be looking into the matter. "Have to be reported, though, sir," the constable mumbled.

"Oh, I'll see to that. I'll have a word with your superintendent later today, sort everything out," said Dennison. "Your local knowledge may be valuable, though, so if we might call on you later?" At which the young constable looked mighty pleased, and suggested that he station himself outside the door.

"No," said Holmes. "It would be much more useful if you were to go to the main desk, and prevent anyone from leaving the hotel."

"What, the guests and all? Begging your pardon, sir."

"We must do so, I fear. If the murderer is still in the hotel, then we do not want him leaving, do we?"

"There'll be complaints, sir," the constable told him.

"Well, if any of the guests insist, refer them to me. Send them up here, would you?"

The constable grinned at this, and set off downstairs.

"Can the poor chap be moved?" I asked, gesturing at the unfortunate Williams.

"I don't see why not," said Holmes, looking a question at Dennison.

"Yes, I think so. And perhaps we can get Miss Blake back to her room?"

Miss Blake protested gamely, but I, being for the moment her medical advisor, lent my weight to the argument, and assisted her to her feet. "I'll let the manager know about … about Williams, too," I said. "I suppose the hotel has its own discreet way of handling these things."

Holmes nodded, and I took Miss Blake to her room, which was on the floor above. I gave her a mild sedative and told her to go to bed, saying that I would look in on her in a couple of hours.

As I made my way downstairs, I met the alert young man who had earlier volunteered his services. He nodded a greeting to me, and asked, "All the excitement settling down now?"

I did not want to give too much away. "Pretty well."

"Is she all right? The lady … the maid, that is?"

"Oh, right as rain. A bump on the head, that's all."

"Jolly good." And he nodded a farewell, turned and went back downstairs, the way he had just come.

I followed, and saw him wander off towards the dining room. I informed the manager that Williams's body could now be moved, and set off back upstairs. It was not until I reached the door of Williams's room that it struck me that the obliging young man really should not have known that any maid, much less any lady, was involved! I hesitated, wondering whether to follow him and question him, or whether to mention the matter to Holmes. Then I shook myself – the young chap must have seen me taking Miss Blake upstairs, of course. And he would, being a polite young man, naturally refer to any lady as just that, a 'lady', rather than merely a 'maid'. I laughed at my own foolishness, and went into the room.

"Ah, Watson. We were just discussing this odd business," said Holmes.

"Odd, in that the body was apparently searched, but the cash left?" I asked.

"That, and other things."

"Nothing odd about that," I said. "The killer knew the notes were fakes, and thus worthless!"

Holmes stared at me in open admiration. "Of course!" he said. "Well, then, Mr. Dennison here tells me that he was informed by means of an anonymous note that Williams was involved in the counterfeiting, and would be here at the hotel last night."

"Well?"

"Well, who sent that note?"

"I don't know! A public-spirited citizen?" I hazarded.

"And who killed him? The same public-spirited citizen? Or was it merely a coincidence, think you?"

"H'mm. No, it was probably no coincidence," I said. "In which case, the sender of the note was also the killer? But why? Why invite the official forces, in the guise of Mr. Dennison here, and the unfortunate Miss Blake, to witness the murder?"

"Witness?" Holmes stared at me, a curious look on his face. "You sparkle, as always, Watson. Now, I wonder ..."

"Wonder what, Holmes?"

"For one thing, I still wonder why the killer, assuming that the killer was involved in the forgery, did not remove the fake notes? Agreed, as you so perceptively point out, Watson, they are not intrinsically valuable; but yet they are evidence, which a clever crook might well have thought to remove from official notice."

"H'mm, yes. Never thought of that," I had to admit.

"And then, if the killer were not himself a forger, but recognized the forged notes, why not take the real money at least? Sixty pounds is a useful sum, is it not?"

I was puzzling over this point when our friend the constable reappeared, to inform us that some of the guests, who had planned to leave that morning, were getting a touch restless. Moreover, the inspector had arrived, and demanded to know what was going on. And for good measure, the local undertaker was here, and would like to remove the body.

Dennison stood up. "I'll sort this out," he told us. "Meantime, Mr. Holmes, perhaps you would like to do some of that theorizing for which you are so renowned?" And he followed the constable out of the room.

"You had best take a quick look at this poor devil, Williams," Holmes told me. "I should judge he has been dead for no great length of time. Meantime ..." and he strode to the old-fashioned wardrobe which stood in one corner of the room, hesitated before it a moment, then whipped open the door.

"Expecting to find the killer still in there, Holmes?"

"Hardly! And yet I fancy that someone may have stood in here, there are recent scuffs on the floor. Most probably done when the maid last cleaned the room, of course, but it does not rule out the possibility that the killer lurked in here. H'mm, possibly he killed this Williams, then heard Miss Blake at the door. He conceals himself hastily, strikes her as she bends over the body, and then completes his search. Yes, that would serve to explain things." He closed the door of the wardrobe. "Have you concluded your examination?"

"I agree with you as to the time of death," I said. "An hour, two at the most, which is consistent with what we already know. A single blow, an ordinary enough clasp knife, Sheffield made."

"A single blow. The killer knew how to use a knife?"

"I should say so." I looked more closely at the knife. "It has a hefty enough blade, four inches long, would you say? Even so, it took a powerful thrust, and some knowledge of anatomy, to do the job with a single blow. An accomplished thug, as I judge. A bad business."

"Anything more, Doctor?"

"Nothing I can see, Holmes. The post mortem examination may show something different, but it looks as if a single knife wound killed him."

"The body is fully clad, you see, and the linen is clean."

"Consistent with the time," I said. "He was most likely getting ready to go for his breakfast, poor devil."

"Yes, it seems certain that he died this morning, rather than at some time last night." Holmes rummaged in his pockets and produced his pipe. "Have you a match, Watson? Thank you. And have you a theory?"

I laughed. "Afraid not, Holmes. Bits and pieces are clearer, though."

"Oh?"

"The chambermaid, Miss Blake, that is. That makes sense, now."

"Indeed?"

"Does it not?" I asked cautiously.

"Why, then, was she so scared when she met you?" asked Holmes, studying his pipe intently.

"Well, she had just … no, she hadn't! I was going to say that she had just found a body, but I bumped into her an hour before that!" I thought. "Well, then, how's this? She was scared because she was keyed up, nervous because she dreaded the task before her. She sets off for Williams's room, then bumps into a complete stranger … damn!"

27

"What?"

"That makes no sense either. Miss Blake said that she did not come to this room until Dennison went down to breakfast, and he did not go to the dining room until we were leaving. The timing is all wrong. And then Miss Blake was not actually going downstairs when I bumped into her! She was going upstairs, up to our floor … and hers … from down here!" I stared at Holmes. "But that would mean that she had visited Williams's room, this room, an hour before all the fuss! But then if she had found the room empty, why did she not search it then?"

"She did not find the room empty," said Holmes, "for we did not see this Williams in the dining room. He must have been here in order to be murdered, as it were."

"Yes, indeed. And then, if Williams were already dead, if Miss Blake had found the body earlier, why did she not report it, if only to Dennison? If she had seen the body earlier, Miss Blake would hardly keep quiet about it. Much less would she go back later to be knocked on the head! It makes no sense. It may have been that she tried the room earlier, but Williams was still in there, so she returned upstairs? That might be it?"

"Then why did she not say so?"

"It may be that this nasty business put the earlier attempt out of her mind, Holmes. Perfectly understandable. That, or else it must have been something else altogether that scared her."

Holmes nodded. "Whatever the explanation, it is clear that Miss Blake has not been entirely honest with us, Watson. And there is another strange point, too. Assuming that whoever killed Williams forgot to search the body … in itself a curious omission, you will agree, when he had gone to the trouble of murdering the man … or assuming alternatively that he was disturbed and hid in the wardrobe, then why, having found Miss Blake here, in his way, and knocking her out, did he carefully move her to the sofa, where she would be comfortable?"

"Well, perhaps he moved her to get to the body?" was the best I could do.

"Oh, that much is clear; but why not simply roll her aside? After all, if he had just killed a man, it is odd that he should suddenly become so very chivalrous, is it not? And tapping the poor girl on the head sits oddly with any notion of chivalry that I ever heard of!"

"H'mm. Almost looks as if the murderer knew, and liked, Miss Blake, Holmes? But then, as you say, why the devil should he bump her on the head in the first place, if he knew and liked her?"

"Ah, there you have me. Whatever the explanation may be, I suspect that Miss Blake is playing a deep game, Watson."

"But she is a trusted government employee."

"According to Dennison."

"Oh!" And as I sat there, staring at Holmes, the door opened and Dennison came in.

Three

Dennison gestured at the body. "They want to take the poor fellow away," he said. "Perhaps we should adjourn to my room?"

He led us to the floor above, and to his room, which was almost directly opposite that occupied by Miss Blake. "How is Miss Blake, by the way, now you have had the chance to examine her properly?" he asked me.

I repeated that my patient was not badly hurt, but needed rest.

Dennison nodded. "I concur. No job for a woman, if you ask me ... though I defer to none in my admiration for the ladies! To be honest, I shan't be too sorry to have you gentlemen working with me." He hesitated a moment. "There will be another member of our little team, later today."

"Oh?"

"Yes," said Dennison. "That local inspector is a determined man, and I had to compromise to some extent with him. He is sending to Scotland Yard, asking for Inspector Lestrade to come along and look into the murder."

"Did he suggest Lestrade, or did you?" asked Holmes.

"I did. I know he has worked with you before, Mr. Holmes, and I know he has worked on cases which impinge upon the government's most delicate affairs."

Holmes smiled. "Lestrade is a good man, and no fool. And as you say, he is discretion itself, when necessary."

"Still, I don't fancy the idea of sitting here doing nothing until Lestrade arrives," said Dennison.

"No, indeed. We three may well be able to carry out some preliminary investigations before ever Lestrade gets down here." Holmes moved to the door. "Have you checked the hotel register at all?"

Dennison frowned. "I omitted to do so," he admitted.

Holmes led the way downstairs and asked to see the register. "H'mm. "Williams, London", I see. Hardly expansive, is it?"

"Probably a false name anyway," I pointed out.

"Very possibly. Well, how about the anonymous note which alerted you to Williams being here?" Holmes asked Dennison, nodding towards the door which led to the lounge.

Dennison produced the note, and Holmes glanced at it, then stiffened. "You see nothing odd about this note?"

Dennison frowned. "It is a fairly ordinary sort of note. Any policeman will tell you that there is a class of person which has what amounts to a mania for sending anonymous notes ..."

"Cranks, in a word?"

"Just so."

"But this note was not sent by any crank," Holmes said. "Watson?" and he handed the note to me.

I read, "'If you want to know about the forged fivers, see Williams tonight', and it gives the hotel's name and address. Unsigned, undated ..."

"It arrived yesterday morning," said Dennison.

"As to its being unsigned," added Holmes with a smile, "I think I could wager a fiver ... genuine, of course! ... upon the identity of the writer."

"Good Lord!" said Dennison. "Do you recognize the writing, or something, then?"

"Do you not?"

Dennison stared at him, but I said, excitedly, "Let me see that note again, Holmes!"

"Well, Watson?"

"If it were not too silly ... Holmes, this is the same writing as we saw in the register. Williams himself wrote the note!"

"Impossible!" Dennison practically snatched the note from my hand, and consulted the register a second time. "Well, but this is ridiculous!" he said with an angry snort. "Williams did indeed send the note himself!"

"But why on earth should he do such a thing?" I asked.

Holmes smiled. "That must be our starting point in any investigation, must it not?" He asked Dennison, "You said the note arrived yesterday morning. Was it addressed to you personally, or to the department, or what?"

"It was addressed "To the officer in charge, H.M. Treasury", and like all such vaguely addressed missives it was opened by the clerk in charge of the registry, and directed to me."

"Just so. So this Williams did not know you, nor you him?"

Dennison bristled at the suggestion. "Of course not!"

"So all you had to go on was the name, Williams, the time, and the place?"

Dennison nodded. "We did not know what to expect, hence the subterfuge with the maid's uniform, the attempt to search his room, and so on."

"And from the wording of the note you assumed that some third party wished to betray this Williams?"

"It was a logical conclusion."

"Oh, I quite agree," said Holmes. "But, with hindsight, it was an erroneous conclusion. It seems likely that, far from being betrayed by some third party, Williams himself was merely extending a friendly invitation."

Dennison frowned, and thought a moment. "You mean that he was offering to tell us something about the forgeries?" he said.

"Just so."

"But why phrase the note in that roundabout way?" I wanted to know. "Why did he not just say, "See me", and sign it with his name? That would have prevented any ambiguity."

Holmes shrugged. "I can only assume that he thought this way was somehow safer. If the note had fallen into the wrong hands, if he were identified as 'Williams', for I am sure that was not his real name, then he could claim that someone else had tried to betray him."

Dennison nodded. "That makes some sort of sense. And of course he could not contact me here directly, for he did not know who I was. He could not know who the department might send, of course. Yes, I follow all that."

"And he was killed to prevent his talking!" I added triumphantly. "Poor devil's dodge with the note didn't help, did it?"

"Was he part of the gang, d'you think?" asked Dennison.

"I tend to think he was," said Holmes. "You may be sure that they are taking no chances, so if he were privy to their secrets, he must have been one of them. That seems to be confirmed by the fact that he had a wallet full of forged notes. On the other hand ..." he broke off and mused in silence.

"Holmes?"

"Yes, Watson. I was merely thinking that it was odd, as we have said, for the body to have been moved, apparently to search it, but the wallet was full of money. I wonder if the body was moved in order to place the wallet upon it?"

"The cash was planted, you mean, in an attempt to implicate Williams?"

"It is a possibility. We must find out, if we can, whether he had the money on him whilst he was alive." Holmes went to the reception desk, and motioned to the clerk. "Did Mr. Williams pay in advance, do you know?" he asked.

"No, sir."

"So you did not happen to see if he had any large sum of money on his person?"

The clerk smiled. "Oh, yes, Mr. Holmes! He asked me to change a five pound note for gold sovereigns, and I could not help but see that his wallet had a great bundle of notes in it."

"Ah! You do not still have the five pound note, I suppose?"

"Yes, sir. It is in the safe here, and I made a note of the number, as usual."

I have said that five pound notes were then a considerable rarity, and I should tell you further that it was quite common for their numbers to be recorded in this way – this in itself should tell you how long ago all this happened! Anyway, the clerk opened the safe, consulted the ledger, and found the note, which Holmes passed to Dennison.

"Fake," said Dennison shortly. He told the unfortunate clerk, "I shall keep this note, which is a forgery."

"But ... I must have a receipt, sir!"

"I'll give you a receipt for the fake, by all means."

"And the five pounds in gold?"

"Lost, I fear." And Dennison led us rapidly away, before the clerk could raise any further objection. "Well," he said, when we had reached his room once again, "that answers one question. Williams was indeed part of the gang, or at any rate he had been. He was quite happy to pass the dud notes, and at the same time he was planning to sell out his erstwhile comrades! A pretty thorough villain, if you ask me, despite all that nonsense about speaking no evil of the dead."

"It looks very much that way," said Holmes. "We have not done too badly with the material at our disposal, I think. We know considerably more about this Williams than we did when we started."

"And we know something else, too," I said. "If Williams was killed by the gang to prevent his betraying them, then if we find the forgers, we shall also find the killer."

"True enough," said Holmes. "Although I suggest we should turn it about, and say that if we find the killer, we shall have a lead to the forgers. And, since we do not know where the forgers might have their workshop, but the murder is here, on our very doorstep, the logical approach is to investigate the murder."

"Not much chance of success, I fear," said Dennison ruefully.

"I should not say that," said Holmes.

"No?" said Dennison. "I am pleased to hear it. I confess that, like the local police, I am a trifle out of my depth, Mr. Holmes. I defer to no man when it comes to identifying

35

forged bank notes, or lead half-crowns. And I have written a small monograph on the techniques used in clipping gold coins; but murder is quite outside my experience. I shall happily leave it to you, and Inspector Lestrade, though I reserve the right to take charge should we succeed in identifying the forgers."

"I appreciate your candour," said Holmes with a nod. "But to return to the murder, or its investigation. First of all, can we eliminate the possibility that the murderer was not staying in the hotel?"

"I think so," I said. "Jolly difficult to sneak in past the receptionist or porter and so on. And then he … the murderer, I mean … would have to consult the register, to see which room Williams was in."

Holmes nodded. "And we must consider the strong possibility that Williams was an alias, one which the killer might not recognize."

"Ah, but the same applies there if the killer were staying in the hotel," I pointed out.

"But at least if the killer were in the hotel then he could follow Williams, whatever name he were using."

"True," I said, "but that would mean that the killer knew Williams by sight. And in that case, would Williams not also know the killer by sight? Let us remember the position of the knife, smack in the centre of the chest. The killer must have walked up to Williams and stuck the knife in, which suggests that Williams did not suspect anything until it was too late. Perhaps the killer was disguised?"

Holmes shook his head. "Too dangerous, a disguise might be seen through. Besides, if the killer spoke to Williams, which he must have done to get so close, surely Williams would recognize the voice of another member of the gang?"

"So the killer was not a regular member of the gang, but recruited from outside, specifically to eliminate Williams? He recognizes him from a photograph, shall we say, or a description furnished by the gang?"

Holmes nodded. "That is one possibility. Another is that this Williams was a fairly lowly member of the gang. He might be known to the ringleaders, without his knowing them. That would obviate the need to recruit an outsider. Of course, until we know more about the gang and its organization, we cannot well speculate as to which is the more likely."

"One important point bothers me," I said. "Irrespective of who the killer was, and whether he was staying here or not, how did the gang know that Williams would be here, and was planning to betray them, in the first place?"

"He may have voiced some doubts about the gang. Or he may have been acting suspiciously," said Holmes. "But the glaringly obvious reason, the strongest probability, must surely be that the gang had intercepted the note. That way, they would know his alias without having to consult the register. That would also explain how the killer found Williams without knowing what he looked like."

"H'mm." There was some logical flaw in this, I knew, but I could not for the moment identify it. "Well, then, and just how does the killer get Williams to let him into the room?"

"Well, the obvious way is for the killer to pretend to be one of Her Majesty's agents," said Holmes with a smile.

"The villain!" cried Dennison.

"Most murderers are, in my experience," said Holmes with every appearance of seriousness. "But it would make perfect sense for the killer to impersonate an agent of the Treasury. For one thing, if the killer could convince Williams that he … the killer … was the person whom Williams was expecting to meet, then the killer might 'warn' Williams that that gang was suspicious, and had sent its own agents; and he might stress that Williams should avoid any contact with any stranger who might seek his acquaintance."

"Me, in other words?" said Dennison. "If only I had not misunderstood that damned note, and got to Williams first!" He made an impatient gesture. "Still, it's too late for regrets now."

By this time, I had recollected what it was that had niggled at me earlier. I asked Holmes, "You mooted the possibility that the gang had intercepted Williams's note? But then why did they not simply destroy it, and kill Williams in some out of the way place? Why run the terrible risks which they did run, following him here when they knew a government agent would also be here, and might already have made contact with Williams?"

"Ah, you ask an interesting question," said Holmes. "And there are some intriguing answers possible. One must be that they wanted to talk to Williams, to discover how much he knew about their operations ... and, more to the point, how much he had already revealed to the authorities, for they could not be sure that this was the first time he had given information away. Another possibility ..." and he broke off, and gazed out of the window.

"Yes?" asked Dennison, who of course did not know Holmes's odd little ways as I did.

"I was going to say that there is an even more intriguing possibility, but I think I must be mistaken," said Holmes in an offhand tone.

I said, "There is yet one more puzzle. Why did the killer not do his worst last night? He must have had plenty of opportunity, why did he not kill Williams after dinner? The body would not have been discovered until this morning, the maids and so on do not go into the rooms in the evening unless you ring for them specially."

Holmes sat upright and stared at me. "It is indeed an interesting question, Watson. And there is one very obvious answer, though it may be incorrect."

"And that is?"

Holmes ignored my question, and got to his feet. "An equally interesting question is, why did the killer not wait until later in the day, when there was less chance of his being interrupted by the maid coming to tidy up the room?"

"Ah, but the longer he left it, the greater was the danger that Williams would contact Mr. Dennison here, and give the game away," I said.

"Fair enough," said Holmes, "but there must be a strong possibility that the killer acted when he did in order that he could leave the hotel before the body was found. Since he knew that the maid would be visiting the room shortly after nine, at the latest, that must mean that he has left already."

"Unless he is a very bold man, and is bluffing it out," said Dennison.

"Agreed. But I suspect he would need to be a very bold man indeed who would stick it out whilst the police are all over the hotel. I submit that the probability is that the killer has left the hotel early this morning." And Holmes led us down the stairs to the reception desk.

"Sir?" said the clerk, warily.

"I wish to know whether anyone has left the hotel this morning, if you please."

"Three gentlemen, and one lady. The Reverend Mr. Tobias Merton, Mr. Fanshaw, Mr. Welton, and Miss Ridpath."

"Thank you. You have a note of their various addresses? And when did they all arrive?"

"Miss Ridpath had been here for two days, and Mr. Fanshaw for a week. The other two gentlemen ... h'mm, they both arrived last night."

"Together?"

"No, separately, sir."

"Thank you," said Holmes, jotting down the addresses. "Have you seen the police constable who was here earlier?"

"The gentlemen from the police are in the dining room, Mr. Holmes," said the clerk, with what I could have sworn was a hint of humour.

"Thank you." We went into the dining room, to find the young police constable there, along with a middle-aged man and two elderly couples. The two elderly gentlemen were both of a distinct military type, and neither was particularly happy about being detained.

As we entered the room, one of them said, "Lord, more of them! And who the devil are you?" he demanded, ignoring the feeble protest of 'Really, Gerald!' from a lady whom I took to be his wife.

"I am Sherlock Holmes, sir."

"Never heard of you."

I liked the man better already! A fine old soldier, the sort under whom I had served in Afghanistan. Holmes, considerably discomfited, said, "There has been a serious crime committed, sir, and we are looking into it. I am sure you would wish to render any assistance you could?"

"Put like that, of course," said the old chap doubtfully. "Don't see what it has to do with us, though. Came here for a week's peace and quiet, and now ..."

"You have been here a week? In that case, we must detain you no further."

"Missed the damned train now anyway!"

"There will be another, Gerald," his wife said firmly. "Come along, and leave these gentlemen to their work."

When they had gone, not without some muttered advice, Holmes turned to the man whom we had not yet met. "As I said, I am Sherlock Holmes and ..."

"And I am Inspector Bates. We have heard of you, of course, Mr. Holmes, and I am not sorry that you were here."

"You have telegraphed to Scotland Yard, I believe?"

"Inspector Lestrade is on his way," said Bates, "and should be here this afternoon. Meantime, if there is anything that I, or Gregg here, or the local force, can do to help, you have but to ask."

"Thank you. I had asked Constable Gregg to prevent anyone leaving, and he did splendidly, although I think we are safe enough in letting those four go. Did you manage to check if anyone else had left today?" he asked Gregg.

"Yes, Mr. Holmes, there were four guests left, clergyman ..."

"We have their names already, thank you."

"And I made a list of the other guests," said Gregg, producing his notebook, "and ticked them off when I saw they were still here."

"Capital! You have all the instincts of a detective," Holmes told him. "And are they all present and accounted for?"

"All but one, sir," said Gregg, flushing with pleasure at Holmes's praise. "A Mr. Peter Berisford. He hasn't paid his bill, or anything, but he seems to have pretty well vanished, can't be found anywhere in the hotel. I tried his room, but there was no answer to my knock. Described by the clerk as 'a well set up young chap, looks a bit as if he was a soldier'..."

"Oh!" I said.

"Yes, Watson?"

"That sounds rather like the young man whom I ran into earlier. You know, Holmes, I was certain at the time that he knew more about this sorry business than he should have."

"You did well to recollect it," said Holmes drily.

"Well, but it wasn't *that* suspicious, and what with all the confusion, it simply ..."

"Just so. Well, if this Mr. Berisford has not paid his bill, then presumably he has not removed his luggage?" Holmes strode back to the reception desk, and asked what room Peter Berisford had occupied. When the clerk told him, Holmes asked, "And has he left his key?"

"No, Mr. Holmes. Must still have it with him."

"I see. But there is a spare, or master key? Thank you." Holmes held the key aloft in triumph, and led us upstairs. He stopped at a door, and knocked upon it, gently at first, then more loudly. There was no answer, and Holmes unlocked the door, then hesitated.

"Think he's in there, Holmes?" I whispered.

"Not alive," he answered, and threw the door open.

I do not quite recall what I expected to see, but there were no surprises, pleasant or otherwise. The room was unoccupied, but there were pyjamas and a dressing gown on the bed, an old leather suitcase on a stool by the door, toilet articles by the wash-stand, the usual signs of occupation that you find in any hotel room. I picked up a silver hairbrush, with the initials 'PB' engraved on it.

"Looks as if he might be back at any minute," I said, replacing the brush on the table. "Perhaps he just went out for a walk? There doesn't seem to be anything suspicious here. Or is there, Holmes?" I added, as I saw him take a slip of paper from a drawer.

"Merely a tailor's bill," said Holmes, pocketing the scrap of paper. "Well, Inspector," he told Bates, "I think we must make a proper search for this man, Berisford."

"I agree," said the inspector. "Come along, Gregg, we'll set things in motion. Rely on me, gentlemen, if this fellow is still in the town, we'll have him. Of course, if he's already taken a train, that will be a different matter."

"And perhaps this might be a good time to look in upon your patient, Watson," said Holmes, as we left the room, and he re-locked the door.

"Yes, I might take a look at Miss Blake, see how she is."

"Would she be strong enough to see a couple of visitors, d'you think?" asked Holmes.

"Oh, I should think so. Not too many questions, though."

I tapped upon the door of Miss Blake's room, and when she called out, "Come in!" I looked in, to see my patient sitting propped up in her bed.

"Are you feeling better?"

"Oh, much better, Doctor." Miss Blake glanced at Holmes and Dennison, lurking by the door. "Please come in, gentlemen. Have you made any progress?"

"We have discovered that a young man named Peter Berisford may be implicated in the murder," said Holmes casually.

Was it my imagination, or did a cloud pass over Miss Blake's face as Holmes said the words? Most likely she did not care to be reminded of the events of the morning, I thought. But her voice was steady enough as she said, "I do not know the name, I'm afraid."

"Oh, that is hardly surprising," said Holmes, "as it was a false name. But fortunately I came across a bill, which has the real name ... Peter Blake."

We stared at Miss Blake, who looked defiantly at Holmes for a moment before saying, "You are right, Mr. Holmes. His name *is* Peter Blake. He is my brother!"

Four

"**Y**ou must realize that this is a very serious matter, Miss Blake," said Holmes.

"Indeed," added Dennison, who, like me, had been temporarily lost for words. "If your brother is implicated in these forgeries, not to speak of a murder ..."

"Oh, but he is not!" cried Miss Blake. "It is impossible that he should be, I am certain of that. And yet ..." and she stopped and put a hand to her brow.

"This has come as something of a shock to Miss Blake," I said. "Perhaps these questions would be better left until she is stronger, Holmes?"

It was Dennison who answered me. "I think not," he said, his voice grim. "Miss Blake clearly knew that her brother was here, in the hotel, and failed to inform me of the fact. That is not in itself a crime, of course, or even suspicious, but since Miss Blake also seems to have been aware that her brother was somehow involved with Williams, that makes the matter somewhat more serious, if not downright sinister."

"I agree," said Holmes, his voice as serious as Dennison's had been. "The sooner you tell us what you know, Miss Blake, the sooner we can free your brother of the suspicions that must naturally attach to him."

Miss Blake sank back into the pillows that propped her up, and gazed down at the counterpane.

"Will you not tell us what you know?" Holmes urged her. "It may well clear your brother at once."

Miss Blake slowly, and reluctantly as it seemed to me, shook her head. "I suppose I must tell you," she said at last, "even though it makes things seem very bad for Peter. Oh, but I am sure that it cannot be as it seems! He would never ..."

"If you could tell us from the beginning?" Holmes put in.

"Well, as Mr. Dennison has told you, we arrived here last night, after Mr. Dennison had received that odd note saying that Williams would be here. As I was downstairs, looking for the lounge, I bumped into my brother, quite by accident."

"You had no inkling that your brother would also be here?" asked Holmes.

"Not the slightest notion. I was surprised to see him, and it was obvious that Peter was every bit as surprised to see me. He grabbed my arm, rather roughly, and took me to one side. He told me that he was here on a matter of business ..."

"He did not specify the nature of this 'business', though?" asked Holmes.

"He did not. And then ..." and Miss Blake broke off.

"Yes?"

"He said that he was using a false name, Peter Berisford, as you already know."

"Did he give you any reason for this imposture?" asked Holmes.

"No, he ..." Again came that hesitation. "Peter is a good man, a good soldier ... he is a captain in a well-known regiment, in barracks just outside London at the moment. He is highly regarded by his officers, liked by his men, but ... well, he can be headstrong at times. Foolish, as young men sometimes are."

"And you concluded that his use of a false name was somehow connected with some ... foolishness?" asked Holmes.

Miss Blake coloured. "To be frank, Mr. Holmes, I rather assumed that he was here to meet ... well, a lady."

"Ah. Hence the false name, of course. And when did you realize that such was not the case?"

"I went to Williams's room earlier than I said, at around eight o'clock."

"You surely went later!" said Dennison.

"I returned later, when you went to breakfast, it is true," said Miss Blake. "But I had been there an hour earlier."

"And why did you not tell me you proposed to go then?" asked Dennison. "It was most irregular."

"And dangerous," added Holmes.

"Oh, I thought I would show some initiative, act on my own, and thereby ... to be honest, I hoped to do well, and thus justify Mr. Dennison's confidence in me."

"I see. You entered Williams's room?" Holmes asked.

Miss Blake nodded. "I set off downstairs, and met nobody, so I felt quite safe. I turned the corner from the landing, and then I spotted Peter. He was just going into what I knew to be Williams's room. Immediately my previous conclusions looked silly, and at once I thought Peter must have something to do with the note, and with the investigation that had brought me here. I was confused, and perhaps a little frightened, as you may readily imagine. I listened at the door, but heard nothing. I tried the door, which was not locked, and which swung open. I saw ..." and Miss Blake broke off yet again, and reached for her handkerchief.

I had to make some protest. "Really, Holmes, this is too much!"

"Thank you, Watson. Yes, Miss Blake, you saw ... what, precisely?"

"I saw ... I saw the body of Williams on the floor, and ... and Peter, bending over it!"

"And doing what?"

"He seemed to be looking through the pockets," said Miss Blake, with some difficulty.

"And what did you do? Or say?"

"I must have made some exclamation, for Peter looked up at once, and saw me. I went into the room, and closed the door. I asked Peter what on earth he was doing."

"And what explanation did he offer?"

"He told me that he had arranged to meet Williams, on a matter of business, gone to Williams's room, found the door unlocked, gone in and seen the body lying there."

"He did not expound on the nature of this business?"

"No, he just used the self-same phrase, 'a matter of business', as he had used to me when I bumped into him yesterday evening, and with as little explanation."

"H'mm. What next?"

"He assured me that he had not killed Williams … that, of course, was the matter uppermost in my mind just then … he swore to me that Williams was already dead when he, Peter, had entered the room. Mr. Holmes, I know my brother. He has occasionally been wilful, silly even, but he has never lied to me. I am certain in my own mind that he had nothing to do with Williams's murder!"

"I am sure you are telling the truth," said Holmes. Which was, you will agree, a trifle ambiguous; but Miss Blake seemed comforted by it.

"And what then?" Holmes went on.

"I told him that I believed him, but that Williams was suspected of a serious crime, and the authorities were already investigating him. I said that Peter must leave the room at once, and that if he refused to do so, it was my duty to report his presence there. He saw that I meant what I said, and I walked with him as far as the stairs the servants use, where I repeated my warning that he was to do nothing which might show that he knew Williams. I advised him to leave the hotel at once. He tried to argue with me, saying that he had not concluded his business with Williams, and wished to do so. But I would not listen to him. I told him that I was already betraying the trust reposed in me by the government, and that if he did not leave at once I should report him to Mr. Dennison. He tried to persuade me, but after a few minutes discussion he saw that I meant it, and he left me and went off to his own room."

"And what did you do?"

"What could I do? If I told Mr. Dennison here what had happened, I would involve Peter. I decided that, as Mr.

Dennison did not know that I had been to Williams's room, I should return to my own room, and when I saw Mr. Dennison I should pretend that the task was too much for me, that I had brooded over it and come to dread it, that I dared not visit Williams's room. That would do me no good with my superiors, I knew that, but it would at any rate prevent my having to go to Williams's room again, or so I thought. I hoped that when the body was discovered, Mr. Dennison would not suspect that either I or Peter had been inside the room, or seen the body, or had anything to do with it."

"So you set off upstairs to your own room, and that is when you bumped into Watson here?"

Miss Blake nodded. "I am so sorry that I did not know who you were, Dr. Watson," she told me. "Had I known it was you … and you, Mr. Holmes, for everyone has heard of you … I should have sought your assistance at once! As it was, I ran up to my own room, and was just about to go back inside, when Mr. Dennison came out of his room."

Dennison nodded. "I naturally assumed that Miss Blake was on her way down to search Williams's room, and spoke to her accordingly, 'Ready, are you?' or some such."

"And why did you, Miss Blake, not give the little speech you had rehearsed, say that you were too afraid to go through with it?" asked Holmes.

Miss Blake looked down at the counterpane once more. "Because it had occurred to me that when Peter spoke of 'unfinished business', he must have meant that searching of Williams's pockets which I had interrupted. I realized that there might be something upon the body which would implicate Peter, despite my efforts to get him out of harm's way."

"Ah! So you planned to search the pockets yourself, remove anything incriminating?"

Miss Blake nodded. "Of course, I could not hope to conceal the fact that Williams was dead, the real chambermaid would find him when she went to tidy the room. I intended to search the pockets, remove any clue as to Peter's being involved, or knowing Williams, then at once inform Mr. Dennison that I had found Williams dead. I should then let Mr. Dennison take charge."

Dennison made a sound indicative of strong disapproval. "Most irregular!"

"I am truly sorry," said Miss Blake. "But I could not think what else to do."

"At least you showed a genius for improvisation, for thinking on your feet," said Holmes, with genuine admiration. "But you had not quite finished?"

Miss Blake shrugged her shoulders. "There is little more to tell. I found the door unlocked, as before ..."

"Forgive me," I said, "but there is one point which even you, Holmes, appear to have missed."

"Oh?" Holmes sounded as if he did not share my opinion.

"Yes. Had the door not been unlocked, Miss Blake, how would you have got in?"

"Oh, Mr. Dennison had provided me with a ... a skeleton key, is it called?"

Holmes mumbled under his breath something which sounded like, "Perfectly obvious!" but I ignored him.

Dennison gave a sheepish grin, and told me, "Reprehensible, I know, but the matter is very pressing, and a little illegality seemed justified for the greater good."

"Pray continue, Miss Blake," said Holmes, with a scathing glance at me.

"Well, as I was telling you, I went in, and bent over the ... the body, you know, meaning to search for anything that might point to Peter. I had not had time to do so, however, when I was aware of someone behind me ..."

"You had not heard the door open?" asked Holmes.

"No."

"H'mm. Did you see who this 'someone' was at all?"

Miss Blake shook her head. "I was about to turn to look, when I was struck on the head. I blacked out, and did not know anything more until I awoke to find you, Dr. Watson, ministering to me."

"But you cannot have been unconscious for very long," said Holmes. "We must have run to the room, having heard the maid ... the real maid ... screaming, only some ten minutes after you were struck on the head."

"As Dr. Watson has said, it is not a very serious wound," said Miss Blake. "There is a nasty swelling ... I must look dreadful! And I have a painful headache, though that is by no means as bad as it was at first. Indeed, the greatest injury is to my pride, for I have not made a very good showing in all this."

"You acted as you thought best, and with no consideration for yourself," said Holmes. He stood up. "Still, serious injury or no, you need rest, as I am sure Watson will agree. Come along, gentlemen, we have much to do."

"And Peter?" asked Miss Blake anxiously. "Can you give me any hope that he has nothing to fear from the law?"

"If he has done nothing wrong, he has nothing to fear," said Holmes, with that same ambiguity which I had noted earlier.

"Then I am satisfied that he has nothing to fear," said Miss Blake stoutly. "For I know that he is incapable of any evil action."

"I trust you are right." And Holmes led us outside.

"And I trust she is, too," said Dennison, in a tone which suggested that he knew his trust was misplaced. He unlocked his own room, and ushered us inside. "Find a seat anywhere, gentlemen. A cigar?"

Holmes produced his ancient briar pipe. "If I may? I find that strong tobacco is conducive to clear thinking."

"If not to clear breathing!" I muttered. I was pleased to see that Dennison opened a window before Holmes lit up.

"Well, gentlemen?" said Holmes, when once his pipe was alight to his satisfaction. "What did you think to Miss Blake's account?"

"It confirmed my worst fears about women in government service!" said Dennison.

"And that important point aside?"

Dennison shrugged. "It shows her brother in a very suspicious light, that much is certain," he said.

"Watson?"

"It rang true, though of course there were great gaps in it. But I am certain that Miss Blake sincerely believes what she told us. She is convinced that her brother is innocent."

"And are you?"

I hesitated, not wishing to seem unchivalrous. "I confess that I must concur, reluctantly, with Dennison. Even if this Peter Blake is not guilty of murder, even if he has no connection with the forged notes ..."

Here Dennison made a noise like, "Huh!"

"... Still, Peter Blake is not what I could call entirely innocent," I finished.

"Hear, hear!" said Dennison. "Although I beg to differ as to the likelihood of Blake's not being involved in either the murder or the forgeries. Are you suggesting, Doctor, that Blake was here on another matter entirely? Why, it would surely be the most monstrous coincidence, were it so!"

Holmes nodded at this. "It was no coincidence, Blake's being here. You recall that Blake himself said ... and this on the testimony of his sister, who is desperately trying to show him in the most favourable, most innocent light possible ... Blake himself admitted that he was here to do business with Williams. It is difficult to accept that such 'business' was entirely unconnected with the forged banknotes, is it not?"

I had to agree that it was unlikely. "But then who tapped Miss Blake on the head?" I wanted to know. "It must have been someone who wanted to search Williams's body; and we know that her brother wanted to do just that but was interrupted! Couple that with the very odd fact of her being moved so considerately onto the Chesterfield, and it rather looks as if Peter Blake went back to finish the job he had started, despite his promises to his sister."

"And knocked his own sister out?" said Holmes, sceptically.

"It wasn't a serious attack," I pointed out. "Not intended to be a fatal blow, by any means, unless I am much mistaken. Why should a murderer, who had just stuck a knife in Williams, cavil at hurting Miss Blake?"

"You have a point," Holmes admitted. "Of course, the other possibility is perhaps the more intriguing."

"And that is?"

"And that is that Peter Blake did not strike his sister."

"And that is intriguing because it raises the question: who did?"

Holmes nodded. "More, it suggests, does it not, that the man who murdered Williams also knocked Miss Blake unconscious? That, or we must postulate an almost infinite number of villains going into and out of Williams's room, like a bad French farce!"

"But why should the murderer … assuming that Blake was not the murderer … knock her out?"

"Clearly, to prevent her finding whatever was on the body."

He had lost me now. "But we know that Blake wanted whatever was on the body! And hence, presumably, he would not wish his sister to find whatever it was?"

"Ah, but you assume that whatever was on the body, or was believed to be on the body, was sought only by Blake."

I frowned. "You mean that Blake and the unknown murderer were looking for the same thing?"

"Is that so hard to accept?"

"But what might this mysterious 'something' have been, Holmes? It was not the money, the forged notes, because if the murderer … oh, very well, if whoever searched Williams's body … had time to move him, and also to move Miss Blake, then the searcher certainly had time to find and take whatever he sought."

Holmes nodded. "It is certainly a pretty little puzzle, and one which I shall think over in my own room." He waved his pipe and laughed. "There is too much fresh air in here for concentrated thought!"

"There is one thing, Holmes," I said reluctantly.

"Oh, I'll open a window if it gets too bad in there."

"No, not that … although I recommend it, of course. No, it was to do with Miss Blake."

"Well, then?"

"I hesitate to suggest it, but may it not be that Peter Blake knew that Williams was here because his sister had told him so?"

Holmes stared at me.

"One puzzle has been that Blake was here at the right time," I went on. "It seems a coincidence, but it cannot be, so perhaps Miss Blake had ... quite innocently, inadvertently, I'm sure ... let something slip?"

Holmes looked at Dennison, who frowned. "I should be reluctant to suggest such a possibility," said Dennison slowly. "But Dr. Watson may have a point. It would explain much, if not all, would it not?"

"Did Miss Blake have any opportunity, between the receipt of the anonymous note and your coming here, to contact her brother, then?"

"I think not," said Dennison. "But we know that she met him here last night, so possibly she said something then? It would, after all, be perfectly natural for the brother to ask his sister what she was doing here."

"True enough," said Holmes. But then ..." and he shrugged. "I shall mull the matter over." And he pulled out his tobacco pouch, and began to refill his pipe in an absent-minded way.

"And what can we do in the meantime?" asked Dennison.

"If you can think of anything that might give us a pointer, pray let me know," said Holmes. He stood up. "And now, if you will excuse me?"

Dennison looked after him as he left the room, then turned to me. "I have heard of Mr. Holmes's methods, of course," he said, somewhat doubtfully as it seemed to me. "But I confess that I cannot see what he might hope to achieve here. It seems clear to me that Miss Blake's brother is somehow involved ... although I hesitate to follow you, Doctor, and implicate Miss Blake to boot. What else can Mr. Holmes think?"

I shrugged my shoulders. "I fear you are right, sir. A pity, for Miss Blake seems a nice girl, and her brother a pleasant young chap. Still who can say?" I stood up. "I think I shall take a stroll round the garden and smoke a pipe. Perhaps that will give me some inspiration. If you will excuse me?" And off I went.

I could not tell you what course my deliberations took, but I did not arrive at any particularly impressive conclusions. I do know that I had more than one pipeful of tobacco, and explored the surroundings of the hotel pretty thoroughly. And I recall that I was ready enough for my luncheon when the hour duly arrived.

Holmes did not appear in the dining room, and I knew better than to disturb his reflections. Nor did I see Dennison, I assumed that he would take his luncheon later, or that perhaps he had gone for a walk and would take some refreshment elsewhere. My own simple meal over, I was at something of a loose end, and wandered outside once more in an aimless fashion. I was somewhat cheered to see a horse and trap roll up to the hotel entrance, and the familiar figure of Inspector Lestrade of Scotland Yard jump down from it.

Five

"**W**ell, Doctor!" said Lestrade, shaking my hand vigorously. "Murder and mayhem follow you like a seagull follows a trawler!"

"It does sometimes seem that way, I confess. Gets so as a man can't take a short holiday without being involved in a serious crime, if not two or three."

"Ah, but Mr. Sherlock Holmes will have solved it already, I expect?" said Lestrade with considerable glee.

I regarded him with some curiosity. "You seem inordinately cheerful, Inspector?"

"Do I? Well, perhaps I can bring a smile to Mr. Holmes's face as well. Inside, is he?" and Lestrade gestured at the door of the hotel.

"Yes, of course, I should have taken you up to him at once. Or will you sign the register first? Are you planning to stay here?"

"Yes, it looks a pleasant lodging. And this is where the crime took place, so it's handy."

Lestrade allowed me to take him through the formalities of registration. He asked for, and was given, a room near to those occupied by Holmes and myself, and I went upstairs with him.

When Lestrade had deposited his bag in his own room, I took him to Holmes's, and tapped on the door. "Lestrade is here," I told Holmes, putting my head round his door.

"Ah, come in, Inspector!" He regarded Lestrade critically. "We try to put a little trade your way, you see. But I observe that you are doing well at the Yard. A successful case just concluded, perhaps?"

"It's true," said Lestrade, trying to look modest and failing dismally. "You'll have been talking to the assistant commissioner, I take it?"

"Not at all. I deduced it. But the point now is this business of the murdered man, Williams."

"Oh, the murdered man, to be sure," said Lestrade, an odd note in his voice. "I looked in at the local police mortuary on my way here."

"Ah, you have seen Williams, then?"

"I've seen the murdered man, right enough. But his name isn't Williams."

Holmes gave the inspector a questioning glance. "And what is it, then?"

"It's Lomax, or rather, it was. 'Lucky' Lomax, they called him. Poor devil wasn't quite so lucky this time, though, was he?"

"I know a chap called Lomax," I said.

"You didn't know this one, though," said Lestrade.

"No more did I," said Holmes. "But I gather that you did, Lestrade?"

"He came to my attention more than once, Mr. Holmes. Mind you, I'm not surprised that you never came across him, even with your knowledge of London's criminals, because he just wasn't in your league. Petty stuff, that was 'Lucky' Lomax. Started as a lad, picking pockets, Later, earning his money in a way a gent didn't ought to, extortion, money with menaces, blackmail ... one or two cases that I knew of, and more that I suspected but where the victims didn't make any complaint ... confidence trickery. Nasty stuff, all of it, but nothing that you'd take serious notice of, Mr. Holmes. Even the courts didn't take most of it seriously. 'Lucky' did six months a year or so back, but other than that it was mostly small fines."

"But never any suggestion that he was involved with forgery?" asked Holmes.

Lestrade shook his head. "Lomax wouldn't be clever enough to forge his own signature," he said. "Mind you, he had been a confidence man, like I said, so I could see him shoving the queer ... that's passing dud cash to you, Doctor."

"He did pass a bad five pound note for gold here, and we found a large sum in forged notes on his body," said Holmes.

"There you are, then. Now, if you could outline the facts of the case for me?" and Lestrade sat back and lit a cigar, listening intently as Holmes told him what we knew about the forged notes.

When Holmes had done, Lestrade said, "It's exactly the sort of thing poor 'Lucky' would get himself into, Mr. Holmes. No surprises there."

"And his murder?"

Lestrade shrugged his shoulders. "Sad, especially for 'Lucky', but not what you'd call entirely unexpected. Bound to happen sooner or later, as you might say. I take it that he fell out with one of the other members of the gang, and got bumped off as a consequence."

"The evidence does seem to suggest that this Lomax was planning to reveal the gang's secrets to the authorities," said Holmes, nodding his head.

"There you are," said Lestrade a second time. "That very neatly gives us the motive, does it not? Killed to prevent him shopping the others. Any suspects?"

Holmes and I exchanged a glance. Holmes said, "A young man named Peter Blake has vanished from the hotel, in suspicious circumstances," and he went on to tell Lestrade about Dennison, Miss Blake, and Miss Blake's errant brother.

Lestrade listened with interest and, when Holmes had done, said, "Well! It looks as if this Peter Blake was part of the gang, maybe the only other member. His sister tips him the wink ... maybe unintentionally, just in the way of sisterly gossip ... and he kills Lomax, also called Williams, to shut him up. That do it, Mr. Holmes?"

"It is certainly one explanation, and admittedly would cover all the facts pretty well."

"The real question, then, is just this: did the sister know that her brother was part of the gang?" mused Lestrade. "By Heaven, I've half a mind to arrest her, as an accessory, if nothing worse!"

I myself had half a mind to think that Holmes would make some protest at this monstrous suggestion, but to my considerable astonishment he nodded his head, and told Lestrade, "I am inclined to agree with you, Inspector."

"Are you, now?"

"Indeed. In fact, I should arrest her at once, not merely in connection with the forgeries, but on suspicion of being an accessory to murder."

"Well," said Lestrade. "It's not often we agree so well from the outset, Mr. Holmes. Hang on, though," he added in a suspicious tone, "you wouldn't be winding me up, would you?"

"Not at all," said Holmes. "Arrest Miss Blake, and ... and this is vital, Lestrade ... make sure that a report of her arrest is printed in the evening papers."

Lestrade thought for a moment. "Ah! I have you, sir. Flush her brother out, is that it?"

"That is it," said Holmes. "If Miss Blake is involved, then you have one criminal safe in custody. If she is not involved, then her brother will hardly let her take the blame for whatever may have occurred."

"If he gives himself up, that will make my job easier," agreed Lestrade. He stood up. "I'll arrest Miss Blake at once."

"She cannot be moved, mind," I told him. "She is my patient, and I'll not permit her to be dragged off to the cells."

"Oh," said Lestrade, winking at me, "if there's a female nurse in her room, and a police constable outside the door, that will suffice, I fancy. Now, if you'll excuse me," and off he went.

"Well, Holmes," I said, "the murdered man, Lomax, as we now know him to have been, does not seem to have been a pillar of the community, does he? Still, he hardly deserved to die like that."

"Yes, Lestrade's summary of Lomax's character was intriguing, was it not?"

"You mean … just what do you mean? That he might have been trying to extort money from Blake, who lost his temper and killed him? Something of that sort?"

"It is a line of thought."

"But would Lomax be doing both? Passing forged currency, and extorting money, I mean? Yes, I suppose he might, a finger in every pie, so to speak. Busy chap, if so."

"It would explain why the forged notes were still on the body," said Holmes.

"But then why was the body searched? Oh, of course …" and I stared at Holmes, who nodded and smiled bleakly. "It's still a motive for murder," I pointed out.

"I am well aware of that," said Holmes in a sombre tone. "But if Blake did not kill Lomax, then logically he should give himself up when he reads of his sister's being arrested." He took out his pipe. "If you would excuse me, Doctor? I still have much to think over."

I left him there, staring out of the window. I found Lestrade, and together we went to the local newspaper offices, in order to break the news of Miss Blake's 'arrest'. An earnest young reporter took down the details, and asked some questions to which Lestrade gave somewhat evasive answers. But the young man seemed more than satisfied with what he called his 'exclusive', using the adjective for a noun, and assured us that the story would be on that evening's front page.

He was as good as his word. Lestrade and I spent the rest of the afternoon at a local inn, smoking our pipes, yarning about the cases we had investigated and the people and places we had known, and I dare say doing a good deal of boastful exaggeration in the process. But as it neared the time when more sober folk are thinking of afternoon tea, we left the little inn and headed down the street towards the hotel.

Lestrade nudged me in the ribs, and indicated a newsvendor. "Looks like business, Doctor."

He parted with his tuppence, and scanned the headlines eagerly. "Done us proud, you see."

I glanced at the paper. "H'mm. 'Dreadful local murder! Scotland Yard make immediate arrest!' Yes, here are the details, 'Miss Amy Blake, sister of Mr. Peter Blake, was arrested on suspicion ...', yes, I think that should do it." And Lestrade and I smiled at one another like a couple of conspirators, and went off to our tea.

The London papers – alerted by the earnest young reporter, whose ambitions were centred upon Fleet Street and a national newspaper – also ran the story in the late evening editions, and those of the following morning.

At nine o'clock next morning, a young man carrying a copy of *The Times* walked into the local police station and asked to see Inspector Lestrade; upon being asked his business, he said he was Peter Blake.

*****

"I never killed Williams, or Lomax, I should call him," said Peter Blake gravely, looking at Holmes, Lestrade and myself. "And certainly Amy ... my sister ... never had the slightest thing to do with the whole sorry business."

"But you must see that things look very grim for you," said Holmes.

"Grim?" Blake looked round the dark and poky interview room in the police station. "I should say so." He managed a smile.

Lestrade began, "This is no laughing matter, my lad ..." but Holmes held up a hand.

"Mr. Blake," said Holmes, "by far the simplest solution is for you to tell us everything ... everything, mind ... that you know about this matter. Any attempt to prevaricate, and things will go badly with you. Now, to begin with, why was Lomax blackmailing you?"

Blake started, then smiled again. "You are close, Mr. Holmes, but not quite close enough. Lomax was not blackmailing me, but a friend of mine, Lieutenant ... well, let us leave his name out of it, shall we?"

"That may not be possible," said Holmes.

Blake frowned. "If it came to it," he said, and shrugged. "I'm sure he would confirm the truth of what I'm about to tell you. Well, he got himself into a corner ... oh, nothing sordid, nothing the Inspector here could lock him up for." He hesitated. "The usual thing ... a woman, of course. Silly young ass," he added, frowning and quite overlooking the fact that he himself was not exactly the 'Old Man of the Sea'.

"There were letters?" said Holmes.

Blake nodded. "This Lomax fellow had evidently bought them from the lady ... who is no lady as I understand the term! My friend's father is one of the old school, strict to the point of severity. Had he seen the letters, he'd have cut my friend out of his will, and that would have been a bitter blow. The amount demanded was fifty pounds, not a fortune, but more than my friend could get together at short notice. Lomax obligingly gave him time to raise the wind, and asked him to meet him ... Lomax ... at the hotel the night before last. My friend happened to be on duty that night, and so he asked me to come along, as I wasn't, and undertake the transaction on his behalf."

"Which you agreed to do?"

"Agreed, and I did it, or at any rate I tried." Blake frowned. "The first thing that went wrong was that I bumped into Amy ... my sister ... in the lobby! I nearly fainted with the shock, the last I'd heard was that she was working in the Treasury, and I didn't want her asking too many questions. I spun her some yarn or the other, and skulked off to my room. I knew which room Lomax was in ..."

"I understood he was using a false name?" said Holmes quickly.

"Yes, that's right. Williams, he'd told my friend to ask for. Well, that was all right with me, made good sense. As a matter of fact, as you've gathered, I was using an alias myself,

Berisford. I wouldn't have bothered to do that, only I knew Lomax was using a false name. All very cloak and dagger. Anyway, I went along to his room, and he let me in. He looked a bit suspicious at first, hadn't expected me, but I told him who I was, explained the situation, and he became a touch less edgy. I gave him the fifty pounds, but then he told me that the price had gone up! He'd looked into my friend's expectations, he said, and reckoned he could well afford another fifty pounds extra. Meantime, he would keep the fifty I'd handed over."

"And how did you react to this news?" asked Holmes.

Blake frowned. "How would you have felt? I wanted to scrag the little rat there and then!"

"And did you?" asked Lestrade quickly.

Blake frowned again, then laughed. "I did not, Inspector. What would have been the point? He might well not have had the letters on him, and if I'd killed him, then some other rotten little crook might have crawled out of the wainscotting, and my friend would be no better off. While if I'd given him the thrashing he deserved, the price would just go up again."

"And so what did you do?"

"Nothing. That is, I told him that I'd pass the news on to my friend, but that the first fifty had pretty well cleared him out, and he would need time. "No trouble, I'm sure", said Lomax with a smirk. "Whenever suits him, suits me", and he ushered me out into the corridor."

"And then what?"

"Then I went back to my room, blazing mad, and smoked about two hundred cigarettes, whilst I thought what best to do. I eventually decided that since I was acting for my friend, I would act as I imagined he would act under the same circumstances. I decided that I would confront Lomax, say that I'd kept my side of the bargain, and demand that he surrender either the letters or the fifty pounds. I hoped that he was so greedy that he would settle for a bird in the hand, take ready cash for the letters, but if he refused, then at least my friend would have the money … because I could foresee that if Lomax got the entire hundred, then he would demand yet more. By the time I'd worked all this out, it was about two in the morning, so I decided to turn in and see Lomax before breakfast."

"Which you did? Or tried to do?"

Blake nodded. "I slept badly, if at all, and was up and dressed at eight or so. I went along to Lomax's room, and tapped on the door. There was no answer, so I tried it, and it was unlocked. I took it that I'd just missed him, that he had gone to his breakfast, but decided to have a look round his room anyway, see if the letters were there. I opened the door ..." and he broke off.

"You saw his body?" asked Holmes.

Blake nodded. "I didn't know what to think. I knew I hadn't killed him. I suppose I rather thought ... insomuch as I thought anything coherently ... that he must have tried the same dirty trick with some other poor devil, and they hadn't been quite as tolerant as I had. Well, it was pretty obvious that I couldn't have helped him even if I'd wanted to, which I didn't, so I thought I might as well take a look, see if the letters were on him."

"You started to search the body, then?"

"I did, but I hadn't done more than tap his coat to see if he had a pocket book on him, when the door opened! I looked up, and there was my sister, dressed up as if she were in some ridiculous charade! Before I could do more than stammer out some nonsense or other, she informed me that Lomax was under investigation by the authorities. I assured her that I hadn't killed him, and she said that she believed me, but that others might not, and that I must leave the room, and preferably the hotel, and go back to my regiment and forget the whole business. I promised her that I would, and we went out into the corridor together. Amy left me, and I stood there, trying to collect my wits."

"And when you had collected them, you returned to complete the search?"

Blake nodded again. "You see, I was thinking about what Amy had said, that Lomax was being investigated. I assumed that she meant with regard to his blackmail activities, and I shuddered at the thought that some clumsy great policeman ... no offence, Inspector ... might rummage through his pockets and find those damned letters. I had to prevent that, if I could, so I broke my promise and went back. Then I'm damned if, just as I'd started again, I didn't hear someone outside! I thought it was getting farcical, but then it might not have been quite so funny if it were the maid or someone, so I nipped into a sort of cupboard thing, a wardrobe or something, and closed the door, but not properly, so I could just see out. I saw that it was Amy, still dressed like a chambermaid, and she was going to do exactly what I'd gone back there to do, and search Lomax! I didn't want that, so I sneaked out, and ... and ..."

"Hit your sister on the head?"

Blake groaned. "I simply couldn't see any alternative, Mr. Holmes. I didn't want her to find the letters, and I didn't want her to find me."

"What was it that you hit her with?" I asked, curious.

"A bag full of clothes, or shoes or something. It was Lomax's bag, in the bottom of the cupboard. Well, Amy keeled over, so I moved her to a couch thing, and got Lomax into a chair, where I could work better. I had to move fast, because I knew Amy wasn't badly stunned. Or at last, I hoped she wasn't."

"You found the letters?"

"And the fifty quid. All of which I took."

"How did you pay Lomax?" asked Holmes. "Gold, or notes?"

"Notes." Blake smiled. "When I saw his wallet, I thought that my guess had been right and he'd been doing a roaring trade, for there must have been a couple of hundred in there, at the very least. I couldn't quite see why whoever had killed him hadn't cleaned him out, but I'd other things to occupy me just then. I took the letters, and my own fifty pounds ..."

"Your own? How did you know they were yours?"

"Because I had the cash in a manila envelope, and it was still in there. Still is," and Blake produced a long brown business envelope. "Count it if you like."

"I won't count it," said Holmes, "but I will take a quick look, if you please."

Blake looked surprised, but handed the envelope over. Holmes looked at each note, then nodded and handed it back. "Those are all quite genuine notes."

Blake looked puzzled. "Of course they are. You didn't imagine I'd pass duds, do you, even to a crook like Lomax?"

"And the letters?"

Blake smiled. "Burned them," he said briefly.

"So there is nothing to corroborate your story, sir?" said Lestrade.

"I prefer to think that there is nothing to cause my friend trouble," said Blake. "Well, Inspector, gentlemen, you have heard my tale, such as it is. I assume I am free to go, and that any charge against my sister will be dropped at once?"

Lestrade looked at Holmes, who said, "Let us not be too hasty." He took out his pipe. "Speaking of burning, I expect it is against the regulations, but I feel the need of intellectual stimulation." He blew through the pipe, frowned, and blew again. "It needs a good clean, I fear." He tapped his pockets. "Does anyone have penknife?"

Blake took a little silver knife from his pocket and handed it to Holmes, who scraped the bowl of the pipe in a perfunctory manner before handing the knife back. "Thank you. It is a nice knife."

"Coming of age present," said Blake. He looked at Lestrade. "Well, Inspector?"

"No more questions, Mr. Holmes?"

"None, thank you, Lestrade."

Lestrade stood up, and Blake made to do the same, only to slump back in his seat as Lestrade cleared his throat, and recited, "Peter Blake, I arrest you for the murder of one 'Lucky' Lomax, real name unknown ..."

Six

"And what do you propose now, Lestrade?" asked Holmes, as we three strolled back to the hotel.

"Well, Mr. Holmes, I think that my involvement ceases here and now. I'll have Blake shipped back to London as soon as possible, under guard, and then take him before a magistrate." Lestrade hesitated, and gave Holmes a sidelong glance. "I must say, sir, that I half expected you to demur at my arresting him!"

"My dear Lestrade, there was no other course you could adopt."

"Then do neither of you believe his story?" I asked, a touch annoyed.

"Do you?" asked Lestrade. "That nonsense about his mysterious 'friend', whose name he won't reveal!"

"Oh, we're all men of the world," I told him. "Of course there wasn't any 'friend', Lestrade! The letters were his own, written by him to the mysterious shady lady. That was why he was compelled to knock his own sister on the head, to prevent her reading the damned things."

Lestrade laughed. "You have an explanation for everything, Doctor."

"And you'll find it's the right one, Inspector! What about the knife? You saw yourself that Holmes ... by a very clumsy subterfuge ... established that Blake still had his own knife in his pocket, so it couldn't have been his knife that was sticking in Lomax's chest."

Holmes shook his head. "The evidence of the knife is inconclusive, I fear, Watson. I examined the murder weapon closely. It appeared to be new, but when I used my lens it was clear to me that it had been sharpened recently."

"Couldn't have been new, then," I said triumphantly. "And nobody carries two knives in his pockets, after all, so that surely lets Blake out?"

"It may have been specially bought, though," said Holmes remorselessly, "and touched up to a razor sharpness precisely to be a more effective weapon."

"H'mm."

"What is more to the immediate point," Holmes went on, "is the matter of the forgeries. You do not propose to look into that, Lestrade?"

Lestrade frowned. "I had thought that Mr. Dennison, as an agent of the Treasury, was in charge there, sir? I have not been invited to look at that case."

We had by now reached the hotel. Lestrade nodded in the general direction of the main door. "I'll have a word with Mr. Dennison, see if he would like me to pursue the matter further, or whether he'd prefer to continue on his own account."

"Do you have any objection to our accompanying you?" asked Holmes. "Dennison did ask for our help … or at any rate he did not refuse it."

"Come along and welcome, Mr. Holmes," said Lestrade expansively. He led us inside, quickly found that Dennison was in the sitting room, and went in there.

Dennison rose to greet us. "I understand that you have found this fellow Blake, Inspector?"

"I have, sir. And I've arrested him for the murder of Lomax, or Williams as he called himself."

"My dear fellow, let me congratulate you!" Dennison shook Lestrade's hand vigorously.

"Thank you, sir. But what I wanted to ask you was just this: did you want me to look further into this matter of the forged notes, or what?"

Dennison released Lestrade's hand, and frowned. "But the matter is surely cleared up, Inspector? You have arrested Blake, have you not?"

"Ah, yes, but for murder, sir, not forgery."

Dennison gave an exasperated snort. "My dear Lestrade, the one is surely intimately connected with the other? Why on earth should Blake kill Lomax, apart from a quarrel over the forgeries?"

"Yes, Lestrade," I put in, before the unfortunate Inspector could answer this, "I should be most interested to know just how you would reconstruct the events of last night myself. For I may add that as soon as Lestrade had arrested him, Blake had at once loudly and vehemently denied murdering Lomax, and then had refused to say anything more, and also refused the services of a legal representative."

Lestrade just stood there smiling tolerantly at this minor barrage of questions. When I had finished, he shook his head rather sadly, and said, "Well, gentlemen, Blake, by his own account, was trying to get some letters from Lomax, who was blackmailing either Blake himself, or Blake's friend … that's a moot point, but irrelevant for the moment. Blake adds that Lomax took the cash he'd asked for, but then bumped the price up, and refused to hand the letters over. By his own account, again, Blake was 'blazing mad' at that refusal. I put it to you, gentlemen: what more natural than that Blake should kill Lomax, to recover both the letters and the cash? Mark my words, that was just what happened."

"Stuff and nonsense!" snorted Dennison.

"I beg your pardon, sir?" said Lestrade, taken aback.

"And so you should! Why, the very suggestion is ridiculous! We now know that this Lomax was here with the intention of seeing me, to betray his comrades in the forgery gang. Are we seriously to believe that Lomax was also here to do further blackmail business with this man Blake? It is ludicrous."

"I did have my doubts," said Lestrade. "But then the story I have outlined to you would cover the facts as I know them …"

"But it doesn't cover the matter of the forgeries, as I say. Come along," said Dennison setting off for the door. Over his shoulder, he added, "I take it there will be no objections to my talking to Blake?"

"No, no," said Lestrade, somewhat surprised.

We followed Dennison in silence as he strode along to the police station. Lestrade ordered Blake to be brought from the cells and taken to the same interview room, and we had just settled ourselves in chairs when the door opened, and a uniformed constable pushed Blake inside.

"Hello, Inspector! Come to apologize for this nonsense?"

"Quiet, you!" said the constable, nudging Blake none too gently in the ribs.

"That'll do, Constable," said Lestrade. "You can wait outside. Sit down, Mr. Blake. Do you know Mr. Dennison, of the Treasury?"

"No. I would have wished to meet you under happier circumstances, sir. Sorry I can't shake hands," said Blake, indicating the handcuffs round his wrists.

"I am your sister's superior officer," said Dennison. "Has she never spoken of me?"

Blake shook his head. "But then she only started work at the Treasury some two months ago, as you must be aware, sir, and I haven't seen her in that time, or not until the night before last."

"Then you will not know that I am investigating some forged five pound notes?"

"Oh, is that what the Inspector and Mr. Holmes were talking about?"

Dennison produced his characteristic snort of exasperation. "The murdered man, Lomax, was … as I am sure you are aware … a member of the forgery gang, and he was intending to turn Queen's Evidence, to 'shop', as I think the term is, the other gang members."

"Oh, Lord!" Blake looked astounded at this.

Dennison went on, "That being so, you will appreciate that anyone who had any contact with him must necessarily fall under the gravest suspicion."

"Yes, I see that. But look here …"

"It seems likely that whoever murdered Lomax did so to prevent his talking to me," Dennison went on. "And since your sister works for my department, and had information which …"

"Oh, I say! Look here, you don't think that Amy …" Blake broke off, sweat visible on his brow. "Look here, I understood that she would be released? I mean to say, I gave myself up voluntarily, as soon as I heard that you had arrested my sister. But I've explained that she had nothing to do with any of this, and …"

Dennison held up a hand. "Miss Blake is still under arrest, and must remain so until we learn who killed Lomax, and how the murder was connected with the forgeries."

Blake stared at him for a long moment, then he seemed simply to collapse. There is no other word to describe it, the colour drained from his face, and he slumped forward. Lestrade got up, looked into the corridor, and ordered the constable to fetch a glass of water.

When Blake was somewhat recovered, he said in a dull voice, "Very well. Write whatever you like, and I'll sign it. Just so long as you let Amy go."

"That's more like it," said Dennison. "Now, you admit that you and Lomax together were producing the forgeries?"

Blake nodded, silently.

Lestrade prompted him, "Sir?"

"Yes."

"Just the two of you? Well, sir?"

"Just the two of us."

Lestrade went on, "And you knew that Lomax was going to blow the gaff? To give evidence against you, that is?"

Another nod. "Sir?"

"Yes."

"And …" Lestrade hesitated. "And the story about blackmail was all nonsense? You killed Lomax to prevent him talking to Mr. Dennison here?"

"Yes, damn you!"

Lestrade stood up. "Right, sir, I'm going to get a sergeant in here to take all this down on paper, and then ask you to sign it. You've already been charged with the murder of Lomax, and that charge will stand, but there may be further charges against you in later connection with the forgeries." He looked at the rest of us. "Gentlemen?"

*****

"A good day's work, Inspector," said Dennison with considerable satisfaction. "There seems no reason why I and the Treasury should appear in this at all. To you alone will go the credit. And, by the way, the one charge of murder should suffice, if he pleads guilty. The less the general public knows about the forgeries the better ... don't want any panic, do we? We still have the quite considerable job of rounding up as many of the forged notes as are still in circulation." And he shook hands all round, and went off.

Holmes took out his pipe, lit it thoughtfully, and gazed at Lestrade. "A good day's work, Lestrade?"

Lestrade did not answer, then he gave a sort of shame-faced grin, and a half-hearted shrug of his shoulders. "Mr. Dennison thinks so."

"And you yourself?"

"Well, Mr. Holmes, there's one thing that does bother me, and that's the forged money that you found on Lomax. If this Peter Blake really had been a forger, along with Lomax, and if he really had killed Lomax, then wouldn't it be the sensible thing for him to take the forged notes? Firstly, because they were evidence, and secondly, because he could easily spend them ... forged or not, there was two hundred quid there. And there was sixty pounds in real money. No point leaving it all on the body. Even Dr. Watson spotted that."

"*Even*, Lestrade?" I began, but Holmes held up a hand, laughing.

"No quarrelling, gentlemen! The point about the forged notes is well made. It was something which bothered all of us, and I confess that I can still see no explanation, save perhaps one."

"And what might that be?" I asked, with perhaps a touch of asperity. "I seem to recall that you dropped one or two hints earlier on, but in your usual infuriating fashion you did not elucidate. Perhaps now is as good a time as any to remedy the omission."

Holmes laughed again, and applied a match to the bowl of his pipe. "Very well, Watson. You yourself mentioned something about Dennison and Miss Blake being there to witness the murder. It may be that the forged notes were left just so as to underline Lomax's involvement with the forgery gang; just so that we, the investigators, that is, should think that he was more important than he actually was. Perhaps even so that we might think that such a large sum of money was all that the gang had produced, and that the gang's entire production was now all accounted for."

"To convince us, in fact ... as it seems to have convinced Dennison ... that the forgery case is solved?" I said.

Holmes nodded.

"But in that event," said Lestrade, "then Peter Blake might be telling the truth. He might have had nothing to do with the forgeries, know nothing about them, just as he said." He scratched his head. "But then ..."

"Yes?" said Holmes.

"But then Lomax must have been a busy fellow!" said Lestrade with a grin.

"To be involved with the forgers; then to betray them to the authorities; and on top of it all to be doing a little blackmail as a sideline, you mean?" said Holmes.

Lestrade nodded. "But then Lomax was that sort of chap," he added thoughtfully. "A finger in every pie, yes, that describes him exactly." He nodded again. "Yes, he could have been involved in all that, no doubt of it. And there was that sixty smackers in genuine cash ... where did that come from, for Lomax wasn't exactly one for honest toil?"

"I wonder?" I said.

"Yes, Watson?"

73

"Well, suppose that Lomax had two separate bits of business in hand. Now, if Peter Blake killed Lomax to retrieve his letters, that's the murder solved ... I can't condone it, but at least I can understand it. But that doesn't solve the case of the forgeries, does it? And Dennison seems to have abandoned that inquiry altogether."

Holmes nodded. "Go on."

"That was it, really. Something nags, I know that something is wrong, but I can't think what. Something about Lomax wanting to grab all the cash he could, money for betraying his comrades, and payment for the letters."

Holmes smiled. "Try this, Watson. Suppose Lomax were involved in a fairly small way with the gang, drawing a regular, but not an impressive salary. He obviously liked money, hence the blackmail, which was quite unrelated to the forgery activities. He decides to sell out his erstwhile comrades, but knows that if they are not all arrested at once, if any escape the net ... and that could easily happen ... they will take a dreadful revenge upon him for his treachery. He decides, then, to meet Blake at the same time as he meets the authorities, to accumulate what cash he can ... hence the rise in the price ... and flee with his pockets full of cash."

"That is the sort of thing I was groping to put into words. It would neatly explain what seemed like the strange coincidence of Blake being here at the same time," I said. "But what did you mean about the rise in price?"

"Well, Blake said that Lomax demanded an extra fifty pounds for the letters, did he not? It is no use blackmailing, or attempting to blackmail, a man who has no money with which to pay."

"That's true," said Lestrade ruefully. "Nobody would ever blackmail us, eh, Doctor?"

"So perhaps Lomax hoped that Blake would have more cash on him," Holmes went on. "Perhaps not so much as fifty, but he could have had five, ten, twenty pounds in his pocket. Suppose that Blake had said, in effect, 'Here is another twenty, will you not give me the letters?' then it may well have been that Lomax would take the extra that was offered, return the letters, and ..."

"And skip the country?" Lestrade finished. "After he had collected his thirty pieces of silver from Mr. Dennison, that is."

"Exactly."

"It would make sense," I said. "It is what I was thinking myself. But then another thought occurs to me. If Lomax were indeed cashing in all his investments, as it were, might he not have asked other 'clients' to call upon him here on the night in question? There were, I recall, three or four guests who left the morning after the murder? And all that real money on him, which so puzzles us?"

"You are right, Watson," said Holmes. He turned to Lestrade. "Inspector, the matter stands thus. If Peter Blake and this Lomax were the only ones involved in the forgeries, if Peter Blake was not being blackmailed, if Peter Blake killed Lomax for a reason connected with the forgeries, then you have your murderer, Dennison has his forger, and there is nothing more to be said. If not, if any one of the conditions which I have mentioned is untrue, then a gang of forgers may still be at work, a murderer may still be at liberty, and an innocent man may be facing the rigours of the law. What say you?"

Lestrade thought, frowned, then ticked off on his fingers. "One, forgeries of that quality would demand more than two men ... or at any rate, more than two if one of them were of the calibre of 'Lucky' Lomax, who was not exactly a criminal genius! Two, I'm unhappy about that large sum in forged cash left on Lomax's body. Three ... well, sir, I can't exactly think of a third point, unless it was Dr. Watson's point about there being two reasons why Lomax was here and not just one. That still remains to be sorted out, doesn't it? Anyway, the first two points are good enough for me. I've charged Peter Blake with murder, as you know, but I can ask to continue the investigation, say that I need stronger evidence." He nodded. "Yes, Mr. Holmes, let's look further into it. I'm your man, sir."

Seven

"It seems to me that there are two quite distinct lines to follow," said Sherlock Holmes. "One is the possibility of there having been further blackmail victims, and the other is the provenance of the forged five pound notes. As to the first, there were perhaps a hundred guests in the hotel, and to investigate all of them would be a daunting task indeed. But there were, as I think Watson said earlier, four guests who left early on the morning that the body was discovered, and it should not be beyond our capabilities to interview each of those."

"And the second line of enquiry? The forgeries?" asked Lestrade.

"Ah, now there I must defer to your greater knowledge, Inspector. The forged notes were of a very high standard, and that is significant."

"H'mm. It's a pity that Mr. Dennison took all the duds for the Treasury," said Lestrade.

"All but this one," said Holmes, producing a sheet of white paper from his pocket, with a flourish like a conjurer producing a rabbit from a hat.

Lestrade grinned broadly. "Concealing evidence, Mr. Holmes? And in possession of forged currency? Very bad. Here, let's have a look," and he took the note from Holmes and studied it closely. "Yes, it is a good effort. There's just a bit wrong down here, in the corner."

"You have sharp eyes, Lestrade," said Holmes with genuine admiration.

"I've seen a few bad 'uns, sir. Mind you, most of them are far more amateurish than this. You'd be amazed what they think they can get away with." Lestrade handed the note back. "Yes, Mr. Holmes, it's a high standard all right." He frowned. "There's the paper, for a start. That looks as if it might be the real thing, if you didn't know better."

"Perhaps it is?" I suggested. "Stolen from official sources?"

Lestrade shook his head. "You may be sure that the Treasury takes good care not to lose any, Doctor! And besides, I think we'd have heard at the Yard if there'd been anything of that sort."

"H'mm, yes, I suppose that's true," I said. "Specially made to order, then, by some paper mill whose owners and employees do not realize that they are doing anything illegal? No, hardly ... the paper is so very distinctive. Well, then, what we might call a private operation, run by the forgers themselves? Would that be too specialized a task, I wonder?"

Holmes nodded. "It is that, or some apparently legitimate paper mill is producing this paper in secret."

Lestrade looked gloomy. "Either way, they won't advertise their part in it," said he. "If we had ten times the number of constables that we do have, I suppose that we might check all the legitimate concerns, but that's about all. And that wouldn't get us anywhere, as we've just said."

"Well, then," said Holmes, "what about the plate from which the notes were printed?"

"Ah," said Lestrade, brightening up at this, "that might be more like it, Mr. Holmes. May I see that note again?" Holmes handed it over, and Lestrade studied it closely. "It is good," he said at length. "In my professional opinion, gents, there are three men who could have engraved that. Only ..." and he shrugged.

"Only?" I said.

"Only, Doctor, Mr. Holmes, one of 'em is dead, one emigrated, for the good of his health, as you might say, and the third, MacNeil, is doing fifteen years in Dartmoor. Been there, oh, nine years, ten, now? About that."

"I see," said Holmes, disappointed. "But then ..." and he broke off, looked at the note again, then asked me, "Watson, have you a five pound note about your person?"

"I think so, Holmes." I took out my pocket book, found a five pound note, and handed it to him. "Genuine, I hope?"

"Oh, it is genuine all right," said Holmes. "That was not what concerned me. No, you see the signature, there?" and he pointed.

I could see the signature, but I could not see what he was driving at. "It is the signature of the Governor of the Bank of England," I said. "Every schoolboy knows that. What of it?"

"Well, but the signature on your note, which is a new, crisp one, is different from that on this forgery."

I took the two notes and studied them carefully. "It is as you say," I told Holmes, "but I confess that I still do not see the point you are making."

Holmes sighed. "The signature on your new note is that of the current Governor of the Bank," he said. "That on the forgery is the signature of the present incumbent's predecessor, who regrettably died some eight years ago."

"I still do not see your point, I fear. Old notes ... genuine old notes, I mean, with the previous Governor's signature on them ... are still legal tender, they still circulate, do they not?"

"But this forgery has not circulated," said Holmes. "It is every bit as crisp and fresh as your new note."

"Well, the forger probably just copied the first note he came across."

"Study the two signatures again, if you would, Doctor. The signature on the forgery, the signature of the previous Governor, is ornate, the handwriting florid, and it is lengthy, a Christian name, a whole cluster of initials representing his many middle names, a double-barrelled, hyphenated surname. By contrast, the signature on your genuine note, that of the present Governor, is a clean script, no Christian name, just two initials, and a surname that is short and sweet. Does no question suggest itself to your alert mind?"

79

I thought for a moment. "Why on earth should a forger bother to forge an elaborate signature, difficult of imitation, when he could forge a short and easy one?"

It was Lestrade who answered me, with a little cry of triumph. "Because when the plate was forged, this new chap wasn't yet Governor!"

"Of course!" said I.

And, "Of course," said Holmes. "The plate was engraved at least eight years ago."

"By MacNeil, equally of course," said Lestrade. "Well done, Mr. Holmes." Then he frowned. "But look here, sir, this is all wrong too. MacNeil was suspected of passing a couple of dud cheques, big ones too, but nothing was proved. In the end he was lagged for passing bad sovereigns, though they were not half bad, as it happens. I wasn't involved in his arrest personally, though I went to his trial out of curiosity, but the inspector who collared him showed me some of his handiwork, and it was lovely. Beautiful engraving, every bit the equal of the Mint, and he'd even invented a special alloy to simulate gold."

"I am sure he was a conscientious workman," said Holmes. "But ..."

"Oh, I beg your pardon, I was getting carried away. I meant to say that in all his misdeeds, he was never once suspected of passing dud fivers. Never charged with that, I'm sure, it was certainly never mentioned at the trial ... though it is a few years ago, as I say, so I would need to ask my colleague if there was any suspicion, just to be certain. Now, Mr. Holmes, that being so, how come these forgeries haven't surfaced before now? As you yourself said, that fake was as crisp as if it had been printed yesterday."

"There are surely two possibilities there, Lestrade. One is that this fellow MacNeil had printed a stock of notes and hidden them away safely, but was arrested before he could begin to pass them. Someone finds the notes squirrelled away, perhaps by accident ..."

"Lomax, perhaps? Or Peter Blake?" put in Lestrade.

"Someone," said Holmes calmly.

"And the other possibility? That MacNeil hid not the notes, but the plate itself, I suppose?"

Holmes nodded. "Again we must postulate some person or persons unknown finding the plate and deciding to go into business for themselves."

"Of the two possibilities," said Lestrade thoughtfully, "I incline to the first. Forgery is a skilled job, in its own way, and it would obviously be much easier to pass notes that were already printed and hidden away, than it would be to start up a press and turn them out. Yes, if the notes had been printed by MacNeil, then even someone as doltish as Lomax might have found them quite accidentally, and set up in business. But then, that might also hold good for Peter Blake? It seems clear that Lomax was not in it alone, for then why should he contact the Treasury? After all, he would hardly want to betray himself, would he? There must have been at least one other in the gang for Lomax to 'shop', must there not? You know, I may have arrested the right man after all."

"It is possible, I suppose," said Holmes with a smile. "But then would Lomax have known where to look for the forged cash?"

"Would Peter Blake? Would anyone?" countered Lestrade.

"You ask a difficult question, Inspector," said Holmes. "If no-one knew where to look, we are to imagine a crook such as Lomax finding this valuable treasure quite by accident, which seems a fairly large coincidence, does it not?"

"H'mm. And I've said before that I don't like coincidences," said Lestrade.

"Tell me, Lestrade, did this MacNeil have any family, friends, confederates?"

Lestrade frowned, as if trying to recollect the details. "I'd have to ask my pal at the Yard," he said, "but I seem to think that MacNeil was pretty much of a loner, he didn't work as part of a gang. No family that I recall, though I'd have to check that too. Friends? There was a lady, if you can call her that, but I think she scarpered when he was lagged, took up with a pickpocket down Pimlico way. No, MacNeil had nobody that I can recall. Why?"

"I was wondering if perhaps some confederate or family member had received the plate for safe-keeping, but fallen on hard times and decided to anticipate MacNeil's release?"

"I suppose that's possible," said Lestrade. "No, I don't think he'd any family. Another crook? Possibly."

"Why not ask him?" I said. "MacNeil, I mean."

Lestrade fairly laughed at my foolishness. "Matter of pride, Doctor," he told me. "MacNeil ... any crook ... would sooner cut out his own tongue than 'peach' or 'squeal' to the police."

"I don't know about that," I said. "I could perhaps understand such reluctance it if were his wife, or a son, for instance, who had begun to circulate the notes, for that would be all in the family, as you might say. But you say that there is no family, which means that it is most likely a former partner in crime. If such a man were circulating the notes, that is surely a betrayal of MacNeil, and MacNeil would see it in that light?"

Lestrade's smile faded, and he looked thoughtful for a moment. Then he nodded, and said, "You may be right, Doctor. If we put it in the right way to MacNeil, he may reveal something useful." He looked at his watch. "No good starting tonight, is there? I think I told you that he was in Dartmoor, and I'll have to get an official order to interview him."

"Could you not start right away?" said Holmes, who has a horror of any sort of delay during an investigation. "You could at least return to London this evening."

"No trains, Mr. Holmes," said Lestrade, with great self-assurance. "And in any case, I was looking forward to dining at the hotel! No, sir, with your permission I'll return to London tomorrow, first thing, or first thing after breakfast, that is to say, get my order, you can travel back at your leisure, and we can see MacNeil the day after tomorrow. Will that suit you?"

"I suppose it will have to do," said Holmes, a touch petulantly. Then he cheered up slightly, and added, "Watson and I can profit by the delay by talking to some of those who left the hotel early on the day of the murder." He took out his notebook. "Let me see, there were four. H'mm, one of them, Mr. Fanshaw, gives his address as Glasgow. He thus had a legitimate reason to use a hotel, as he was a long way from home."

"But Lomax might have ordered him to be here?" I objected.

"But you recall, do you not, that Fanshaw had been at the hotel a full week. That suggests strongly that he was here on holiday, does it not? And then how could Lomax have obtained a hold over anyone so very far away from London? Lestrade?"

Lestrade shook his head. "Lomax was no great writer, Mr. Holmes. And anyway he wouldn't trust any blackmailing threats to the Post Office, he'd want to see his victim in person, or slip a little note through their letterbox. No, you can scratch Mr. Fanshaw for now."

"I hoped as much, though we may need to see him later, perhaps. Dear me!" Holmes looked at his notebook again. "Mr. Welton gives his address as London, far enough away to justify the expense of an hotel, but on Lomax's doorstep, so to speak. We must see Mr. Welton. But the two really interesting names are Miss Ridpath, who lives a mere fifteen miles away, and the Reverend Mr. Tobias Merton, who lives only twenty miles off. Now, why should either of them go to the expense and trouble of staying at an hotel, and for so short a time, one night for the Reverend Mr. Merton and two for Miss Ridpath, when their homes are so very close?"

"You can't suspect a vicar!" I said.

Holmes looked mournful. "Have you not read any Sunday papers recently, Watson? Still, we shall make careful enquiries tomorrow."

*****

"Ah, yes," said the Reverend Mr. Tobias Merton, the next morning. He was an elderly man of respectable appearance, though at the moment he looked quite shamefaced. "It was an extravagance, I confess, but I had an early appointment with the bishop, you see. As you gentlemen will be only too well aware, we are rather isolated out here, and there was no suitable train which I could have taken that morning, and so I booked a night at the hotel. And, I must say, I was made very comfortable. Was there anything else you wished to know, Mr. Holmes?"

*****

Sherlock Holmes tapped at the door, which was opened by a pert little parlour maid. "Miss Amelia Ridpath?"

"Please come in," and the maid opened the door wider for us.

Holmes handed the maid his card, and she led us into a room as sparsely furnished as any bachelor's apartment. A strikingly handsome woman, some thirty years of age, and with long reddish-brown hair, rose to greet us.

"Mr. Sherlock Holmes, madam, and - "

"Dr. John Watson, madam," I finished.

"Mr. Holmes," said she, holding out a hand. "I have heard of you, of course. And Dr. Watson," and she shook my hand as well, with a grip as firm as that of any man. "I am Amelia Ridpath. Please take a seat. A cigarette?" and she held out a silver box.

"Thank you, no," said Holmes. "But ... if I may?" and he held up his ancient pipe.

"Feel free." Miss Ridpath herself lit a cigarette, whilst I declined to smoke at all, feeling vaguely that it was wrong for a lady to behave in this fashion – *eheu, fugaces* as my old Classics master would have said, how very long ago it all was!

Miss Ridpath regarded me with a mixture of amusement and mild contempt, though amusement perhaps predominated. "The new woman, Dr. Watson," she told me.

"H'mm. The old one was quite good enough for me, Miss Ridpath, to speak plainly."

Miss Ridpath laughed aloud. "Well, I am certain that you did not come all this way to see me just to discuss politics, gentlemen. Tell me, is it this dreadful murder that I have seen noted in the press? Or is it simply that Hugo's family want to know about those letters?"

Holmes frowned." It is indeed in connection with the murder, as you correctly deduce," said he. "As to the 'letters' of which you speak, I fear that you have lost me."

"Dear me! And I thought Mr. Sherlock Holmes would know everything!"

Holmes smiled. "Not quite everything. Though it is not too difficult to work out that you were being blackmailed by the murdered man, Lomax, or Williams as he was calling himself. Presumably this Hugo is your fiancé, and Lomax was threatening to send him some letters which you had written to a former lover?"

Miss Ridpath nodded. "I was a foolish young girl when I wrote those letters. Oh, not foolish because of the sentiments expressed in them, but foolish to think that the man to whom I sent them would destroy them, or at least keep them private. Hugo would probably laugh the letters off for what they really were, but his family, particularly his mother, would take a dim view of them. Either the marriage would be called off, or poor Hugo would be cut off with the proverbial shilling."

"I see. And presumably Lomax told you to be at the hotel on the night in question? Yes. And how much did he want for the letters?"

"Fifty pounds, at first. He then tried to get me to pay more, but I showed him my purse … which I had taken the precaution of emptying … and told him that there was no more."

"And how did he respond to that?"

Miss Ridpath smiled. "At first he seemed disinclined to hand the letters over. But I threatened hysterics, and that soon made him change his tune."

"You paid him in five pound notes?"

"Why, yes. Safer and lighter than gold."

"Of course. And then you left the hotel next morning?"

"I wanted to get back home. Of course, when I saw the newspapers, I did not know what to think. I was not too unhappy that Lomax had got his just desserts. And I was happy enough to think that the murderer had taken my fifty pounds, for I assume that he did so, because I would gladly have paid that amount or more to see Lomax dead. There is no virtue in hypocrisy, after all. But then when I thought about it more rationally, I was afraid lest my connection with the man might be brought to light … as indeed it has been, now."

Holmes waved a hand. "If you had nothing to do with the murder, you have nothing to fear from me."

"But, Mr. Holmes, you cannot think that I …"

"When did you speak to Lomax, pay him the money?"

"The night before his murder, after dinner."

"And you did not see him again after that?"

"No."

"And where are the letters now?"

"Ah, that is a metaphysical point, Mr. Holmes. I burned them." Miss Ridpath pointed to the hearth. "Of course, Mary Jane has cleaned the grate since my little conflagration."

"Yes, of course." Holmes stood up. "Well, I think that is all for the moment, though it may be necessary to speak to you again."

"One moment," I said. Holmes looked at me, but I addressed Miss Ridpath. "You spent two nights at the hotel, madam. I merely wondered why you were there the night before you met Lomax?"

"Oh, that is easy enough. I decided that since the excursion was going to cost me fifty pounds anyway, I might as well combine business with pleasure, so to speak."

"I still do not follow you, Miss Ridpath," I said.

Miss Ridpath smiled sweetly. "It is very simple, Dr. Watson. The town has some nice little dressmakers and haberdashers. I went down a day early so that I could do some shopping!"

Eight

"Everyone one meets seems to be burning papers these days!" I complained as we made our way to the railway station. "I feel quite left out."

"The penalty you pay for a clear conscience," said Sherlock Holmes with a laugh. "But at least you can sleep easy o' nights, Doctor. Tell me, what do you think to Miss Amelia Ridpath?"

"Her story rang true."

"You do not see her killing Lomax, then? Despite the fact that she is a physically fit, healthy specimen of the new woman?"

"Oh, I'm sure that she is physically capable of killing a man, and that she would have no strong moral objection to sticking a knife into a man who had wronged her. But I know this much, Holmes ... if Miss Ridpath had killed Lomax, she would never have left her fifty pounds on his body!"

Holmes laughed again. "You are almost certainly correct. Which means that Mr. Welton must claim our attention next." He glanced at his watch. "We perhaps have time for a quick luncheon, then we can get a train to London, call upon Mr. Welton this afternoon, get a good night's sleep back at Baker Street, and off to Dartmoor with Lestrade tomorrow."

*****

I enjoyed my luncheon at the hotel, though Holmes fretted in his usual way, and scarcely did justice to the splendid food on his plate.

"Shall we return to the hotel when our investigations in London and on Dartmoor are concluded?" I asked him when we had finished.

"Oh, I think so. I shall tell them that we shall be away one night, perhaps two, but to keep the rooms for us. After all, we have scarcely begun our holiday as yet."

"That is all too true!" I said, with some feeling. "We have been busier here than ever we were back in Baker Street!"

We caught our train, and arrived in London at about the hour when honest folk are thinking of afternoon tea. Holmes had no thought for such civilized amenities, though, and hailed a cab at once.

The Mr. Welton whom we sought had given a business address in the City, and we reached the tall old building just as the homeward bound clerks and stockbrokers began to throng the streets.

"Have we left things too late, Holmes?"

He gave a little grunt of annoyance. "I suspect that we may have done just that, Watson. Still, we may be able to obtain his home address," and Holmes pushed the heavy wooden door open and went inside.

An elderly man, in the unofficial City uniform of black coat and pinstriped trousers, was on his way out, and he gave us a questioning glance. "Gentlemen? I fear that the office is on the point of closing, but if you have urgent business, I am the chief clerk, Augustus Silverton."

Holmes held out a hand. "My name is Sherlock Holmes, sir, and I was looking for a Mr. Welton, who is, I understand, an employee of your firm."

Mr. Silverton frowned. "I have heard of you, Mr. Holmes, and whilst I am naturally delighted to meet you in person, I should be sorry to learn that any employee in this office had come to your professional attention." His face cleared, and he even managed a smile. "However, such is not the case, sir. I fear you have been misinformed in this instance, for there is no-one here by the name of Welton."

Holmes's face fell. He produced his notebook, and flipped over the pages. "Ah, yes. Here is the description of Mr. Welton, as furnished by the receptionist at the hotel where he stayed: 'Thirty-five or so, dark hair, thin moustache, waxed at the tips, black eyes, slight scar over one eye, but not sure which' ..." he broke off and glanced at Mr. Silverton, who had started visibly. "Well, sir?"

"Well, Mr. Holmes, that sounds remarkably like our Mr. Mowbray. The owner." Mr. Silverton hesitated.

"His name does not appear on the plate outside the door," said Holmes.

"No, sir, it is an old-established firm, and Mr. Mowbray joined us comparatively recently. A mere six or seven years ago."

"And is Mr. Mowbray in the building at the moment, do you know?" asked Holmes.

"No, sir, he left half an hour since." Again Mr. Silverton seemed to hesitate. Then he nodded towards the door, and said, "There is nobody else in the office, gentlemen, and I must lock up. But if you have a moment, perhaps we might have a short talk?"

As Mr. Silverton busied himself locking the doors, I told Holmes in an undertone, "The alias was evidently suggested to Mr. Mowbray by his own name. Melton Mowbray, Holmes! Only Melton would have been too obvious, hence Welton, of course."

"A masterpiece of elucidation, Watson. Ah, Mr. Silverton, are you quite ready?"

"I am, sir."

Mr. Silverton led the way to an old hostelry at no great distance from his office. He was evidently well known there, for the barmaid handed him a full glass as soon as he reached the bar. "Gentlemen?"

We found seats in a quiet corner, and Mr. Silverton set his glass down untasted. "Now, Mr. Holmes. I take it that your interest in our Mr. Mowbray is indeed professional?"

Holmes nodded. "If he is the man I seek, then he has been using a false name, if nothing else. Not in itself illegal, of course, but suggestive."

Mr. Silverton took a sip of his beer, but said nothing.

Holmes went on, "So that anything you can tell me might prove extremely useful, sir. I appreciate that you feel a certain loyalty ..."

"Loyalty?" Mr. Silverton interrupted, with as fine a sneer as ever I saw and heard a man produce. "Any loyalty I may once have had towards the firm has disappeared in the last five years, Mr. Holmes, since Mowbray took over."

"Ahah!"

"In point of strict fact," Mr. Silverton went on, "I am about to hand in my notice."

"To resign, rather than to retire?" said Holmes. "Forgive me, but I should have thought ..." and he broke off and stared at the table.

"You would have thought that a man my age would know better, eh?"

"I did not say so. But, yes, you must be close to the time when you would qualify for your pension, must you not?"

"Another couple of years, Mr. Holmes," said Mr. Silverton with a nod. "But I can't stick it out, sir, and that's a fact. I don't deny that things might be difficult, but then I've been thrifty, made a few judicious investments on my own account, so I'm not short of a bob or two. The pension would've been nice, icing on the cake, as they say, but it isn't essential. I've talked it over with Violet ... that's Mrs. Silverton, of course ... and she agrees. Not that I told her the whole story, you understand."

"Indeed. You have not yet told us the whole story, though," Holmes pointed out.

"Ah, yes, I was forgetting." Mr. Silverton looked round, and lowered his voice. "The fact is, Mr. Holmes, that I suspect that Mr. Mowbray has not always been entirely honest with his clients."

"Embezzlement, you mean?"

"I do, sir. And I happen to know that old Mr. Joshua Strang suspected as much, too, for I once overheard him talking to Mr. Mowbray, asking for an explanation something or the other."

"And did you also overhear Mr. Mowbray give any explanation?"

Mr. Silverton shook his head. "No, sir. Except that he laughed it off, or tried to. Said, 'I'll tell you the whole story later', or some such. Only he couldn't."

"Oh?"

"No, because a day or so later, old Mr Joshua died, sudden."

"Ah!"

"Just what I said to myself, Mr. Holmes," said Mr. Silverton, nodding his head. "But what would have been the use of my saying anything, I ask you? Old Mr. Joshua was very old, seventy-three, and the doctors were all satisfied that it was all above board. Mr. Mowbray had been a junior partner, nothing more, but then he bought Mr. Joshua's share of the firm, for less than it was worth, if you ask me, but the heirs were happy enough, a nephew and niece with no interest in business, and I kept my mouth shut. No hard evidence, you see."

"And the firm has prospered, since Mr. Mowbray took over so conveniently?"

"Well, sir, I am bound to say that it has," said Mr. Silverton, with some reluctance.

"No hint of anything untoward more recently?"

"No, sir." Mr. Silverton hesitated once more.

"And yet you feel compelled to resign, to forfeit your pension?"

Mr. Silverton shrugged. "It is a matter of pride, Mr. Holmes."

"And nothing more?"

"Well, sir, if you insist upon it, there was something more. It's this way. Four or five weeks ago, Mr. Mowbray got a letter, at the office. It was marked 'Personal', so I passed it on to him unopened. Five minutes later he shoots out of his

91

office, with a face like I don't know what. Angry? I should say so. 'Silverton', he says to me, 'where are those papers from old Mr. So-and-so's account, five years back?' Well, I looked at him, and I told him straight, 'Mr. Mowbray, you yourself took those old papers, and more besides, from the filing cabinet and destroyed them', and so he did, Mr. Holmes, though by rights they should have been kept until the clients had died, or moved to another house. But take those old records he did, himself, and he burned them, too, for the cleaner told me that she found a heap of ashes in his grate, and that in the middle of summer!"

I dug Holmes viciously in the ribs at this revelation of yet another celebration of combustion.

"And you suspect that these old records would have proved that Mr. Mowbray had acted improperly?" said Holmes.

"Suspect? Nay, say rather that I know it," said Mr. Silverton.

Holmes gave him a quick glance. "Indeed?"

Mr. Silverton looked round the room once more in a very conspiratorial fashion, then took a long manila envelope from an inside pocket. "Indeed, Mr. Holmes. You see, when Mr Mowbray said what he did say about the old records, I waited until everyone had left the office and then I took a little look at the files on my own account, not for one moment expecting to find anything, you know, but just out of curiosity. And blow me if I didn't find something interesting after all! Tucked away at the back of a couple of the old petty cash books, I found … these," and he passed the envelope across to Holmes.

Holmes opened the envelope and took out a thin sheaf of yellowing business papers. He glanced through these, then replaced them in the envelope. "I must confess, Mr. Silverton," said he, "that amongst my talents I cannot number the ready interpretation of stockbroker's memoranda. But these would appear to relate to transactions carried out on behalf of a Mr. …"

"No names, Mr. Holmes! Not out loud, if you please," said Mr. Silverton. He took the envelope from Holmes, and fanned out the documents contained within it. "Now, sir, the old gentleman that's named in there was what you might call a cautious investor, didn't want to take any risks with his money. And this is the official record of a purchase made for the gentleman concerned, a copy of which was sent to him. As you may clearly see, the security concerned is four per cent Consolidated Loan Stock, a very safe government stock. All perfectly safe and sound, as you might say, and the right sort of investment for such a cautious gentleman. However, this ..." and he held up another piece of paper, "is another record of a purchase, same date, same client, but for shares in a Venezuelan railway company."

"I heard there was a big scandal over the Venezuelan railways," I exclaimed. "A pal of mine got his fingers burned rather badly when they crashed."

Mr. Silverton nodded sagely. "That's so, Dr. Watson, and a lot of people did the same. But before they crashed they soared in a quite spectacular fashion. As you may see for yourself from this next contract note, which shows a sale of the railway stock for five times the purchase price, and that within a mere ten days!"

"Brilliant investment management, I'd have said."

"Oh, you could not argue otherwise, Doctor, it's a fact. But then this next note shows a purchase of Consols ... Consolidated Loan Stock ... for the same client. What do you say to that?"

"Only that I'm puzzled," I said frankly.

But Holmes nodded. "The first purchase of government stock never took place," he said. "The contract note showing that it was bought was a fake, sent to the client to allay his suspicions. Mowbray speculated in the riskier stock with the client's money, then when the stock soared he sold out, and really did buy the government stock which the client had ordered, but pocketed the difference, some four times the client's investment. Is that right?"

Mr. Silverton nodded his head with great glee. "You have it, Mr. Holmes! Speculating with the client's money, that's it exactly."

"He did rather well, though," I said. "Of course, a risky stock like that, it could have gone wrong … just as it did for my friend and the other poor fools who didn't get out in time. Suppose Mowbray had done the same, that he'd bought high and then sold low after the crash? He could hardly have bought the genuine safe stock for the client then, could he? What then?"

"Ah, there you ask a significant question, Doctor," said Mr. Silverton. "What then, indeed? As things were, of course, that question was never asked, for it never needing asking. The clients all got back their money, as I take it, but not the enormous profits that they should have had. Thus you might say as they were cheated, but on the other hand none of 'em actually had any cause for complaint."

"And you think that the other records, those which Mr. Mowbray destroyed, would be similar to these?" said Holmes.

"I do, sir."

"And the mysterious note which arrived for Mowbray at the office?"

Mr. Silverton shook his head. "Something to do with it, that much is clear, but I can't think just what. Someone found out and complained, perhaps? Some query about some deal done five years back, that he couldn't answer? Something on those lines, at any rate, or I'm much mistaken. Something that upset him, rattled him pretty badly, I do know that for sure," he added with a grin.

"I'm sure you are right," said Holmes. He tapped the envelope. "May I keep these papers? I promise you that if I need to use them, your connection with the matter will not emerge."

"Oh, I don't care," said Mr. Silverton. "As I say, I'm handing in my notice anyway. Do what you like with the papers. I'd like to see the rascal get what's coming to him, even after all this time."

"Tell me," I said, "you said that since taking sole control of the business Mowbray has not done anything that you would call unethical?"

"Not him. The later records are all on file, all above board, would stand any inspection you care to name. But what of that, if the cash with which he bought the firm was obtained dishonestly in the first place?"

"H'mm. But, apart from these early transactions of a dubious nature, none of his clients has real cause for complaint?"

Mr. Silverton considered this. "No, I suppose they haven't. And even in the early days, if the clients had been a bit more adventurous, he'd have made their fortunes for 'em. Mowbray's shrewd and sharp, all right. The trouble is, he's just a bit too shrewd and too sharp for my taste, if you follow me."

Holmes stood up. "Thank you, Mr. Silverton, you have been a considerable help. I shall not keep you from your supper any longer, sir. Come along, Watson," and he shook Mr. Silverton's hand and led the way outside.

The streets were less crowded now, just a few folk who had been working later than the rest. I said, "Speaking of supper ..."

Holmes waved this away. "You see the significance of what we have just discovered, Watson?"

"Indeed. This Mowbray had his fingers in the till, and Lomax somehow got wind of it, perhaps found another document that had been overlooked, or perhaps met a disgruntled former employee of Mowbray's, something on those lines. He blackmails Mowbray, gives him the standard instruction to be at the hotel on the night of the murder. How's that?"

Holmes nodded. "But then Miss Ridpath paid Lomax fifty pounds, did she not? Peter Blake took back his, or his friend's, fifty. And Lomax had a couple of hundred in forged money."

I frowned. "So?"

"So, what happened to the money which Mowbray was to have given Lomax? Discount the cash which I have just

95

mentioned, and Lomax had around ten or fifteen pounds on him. Hardly the amount I should ask for the return of papers proving that a stockbroker had cheated his clients."

"Oh! You mean that instead of handing over hard cash, Mowbray gave Lomax a knife in the chest?"

"It is a strong possibility, is it not? And there is another point, Watson. It may not have been the business irregularities which formed the subject of the blackmail threat."

"No? Oh, you mean the sudden death of the senior partner, which prevented Mowbray's having to answer some awkward questions?"

Holmes nodded. "A man who has already committed one murder may be quite likely to commit a second, in order to prevent detection."

"Lord, yes. We had better share this latest news with Lestrade, then?"

"We shall see him at once."

"Of course, this still doesn't help with the forgeries, does it?"

"One thing at a time, Doctor," said Holmes with a smile.

Nine

"**M**r. Mowbray?" asked Lestrade.

"Yes, but I was just going out to dinner, so ..."

"Police, sir. I'm Inspector Lestrade of Scotland Yard, and these two gentlemen are Mr. Sherlock Holmes, and Dr. Watson. Shall we talk about it here on the doorstep, or would you prefer a more private chat at the police station, sir?"

"No. No, come in, I mean," and a somewhat chastened Mr. Mowbray led us into his study, and waved us to chairs. "Now, gentlemen, what can I do for you?"

By way of an answer, Holmes took out the manila envelope which Mr. Silverton had given him, and passed it to Mowbray. "Do you recognize the papers in there, sir?"

Mowbray took the documents from the envelope, glanced through them in an indifferent fashion, then returned them to Holmes with a shrug of the shoulders. "Well, they are old contract notes, relating to bargains done some five years past. What of it?"

"It has been suggested that these documents prove that you embezzled ... or shall we say rather, diverted ... monies entrusted to you by your clients. What do you say to that?"

"I say it's nonsense," said Mowbray. He took a cigarette from a silver box, lit it nonchalantly, and almost as an afterthought offered the box to us. "You say it has 'been suggested', Mr. Holmes? May I ask, by whom?"

"That's neither here nor there," said Lestrade.

"Was it old Silverton? I'll bet it was! I'm not surprised, mind you, for the old rogue has had it in for me ever since I joined the firm. In fact, I only tolerate him for the sake of Mr. Strang, the former senior partner. I understand that Silverton is thinking of chucking it in, and it's none too soon, for my patience is running out, and I was thinking of giving him the sack anyway."

"Be that as it may, Mr. Mowbray, how do you explain these documents?" said Lestrade.

"All these documents prove is that I bought two batches of Consols, and bought and sold stock in a South American railway concern at a handsome profit."

Lestrade put in, "And would the client named in these documents confirm that if I asked him, sir?"

"He's not in a position to confirm anything, I regret to say. He died a couple of years ago."

"But his heirs might have copies of these contract notes?" said Holmes quickly.

Mowbray shrugged his shoulders. "If so, their copies would merely confirm the deals recorded here, so that would not substantiate your allegations. Your slanderous allegations, I might call them."

"But if the contract notes relating to the Venezuelan transactions were missing?" Holmes went on.

"Again, what if they were? Clients sometimes discard, or lose, documents. The absence of a contract note is no proof that the bargain never took place. You do realize that I hope, Mr. Holmes?"

From the look on Holmes's face, it was clear that he did.

Mowbray went on, "I wish you would speak to my clients, in fact. They would, to a man ... not to speak of the widows and orphans ... tell you that none of them have ever lost money dealing through me. I will not deny that many of them have an over-cautious approach, which I have tried to talk them out of, but that is their affair. Had they followed my advice, they'd probably have been much wealthier than they are now, but they haven't lost money, any of 'em, and they'll confirm that if you ask."

Lestrade said, "And then there's the matter of the sudden, and highly convenient, death of your erstwhile partner, Mr. Joshua Strang. What about that?"

"What about it, Inspector? I regretted old Mr. Joshua's death … I really did, for he taught me a lot, though he was a touch fuddy-duddy in his approach to selecting investments. But he was over seventy, so it wasn't entirely unexpected or 'sudden', as you put it. As to its being somewhat convenient, I won't deny that it enabled me to buy out his heirs, a feather-brained girl and a silly ass of a young man, neither of whom had the slightest interest in the firm, but merely wanted what cash they could lay their hands on. True, I got the business for about half its true worth, but then they were happy enough, and no man of sense pays more than he need, no businessman is under any obligation to transact a deal to the benefit of the other party."

"So if I were to get an exhumation order for old Mr. Strang, you wouldn't be bothered at all?" said Lestrade casually.

"Of course I'd be bothered! I never heard such arrant nonsense in my life! Why disturb the old chap's rest, and upset the family, such as it is?"

"Did you know, Mr. Mowbray, that our chemists can detect poisons like arsenic or strychnine in a body for decades after it's buried?" asked Lestrade.

"No, I didn't, and I must say that the information, though mildly interesting, moves me not in the least. The only part of your statement that does interest me is the implied slander."

Lestrade held up a hand. "I'm implying nothing, not as yet, Mr. Mowbray. But if our people were to look at old Mr. Strang, they wouldn't find arsenic or anything, then?"

"How should I know what they might find? But I can tell you this, if they found enough arsenic to sink one of the new battleships, I didn't put it there!" said Mowbray. "In fact, I'd rather like you to exhume the body, Inspector. I've half a mind to see the Assistant Commissioner, to insist on an exhumation, then I'd have some grounds for an action for slander."

Lestrade looked at Holmes, as if for guidance.

Holmes said, "Let us try another tack, Mr. Mowbray. Have you read in the newspapers of the death of a man called Lomax, or Williams, at a certain hotel, by any chance?"

"I did read something of the kind," said Mowbray, with an attempt at nonchalance that was not entirely convincing.

"I believe that you knew Mr. Lomax, or that you had some acquaintance with him, at least?"

"Not at all, Mr. Holmes. You're wrong there."

"Ah, but you know the hotel, I think?"

"I have stayed there," said Mowbray.

"Just so, in point of fact, you were there on the night of the murder, were you not?"

"No! You'll not find my name in the register for that night, Mr. Holmes."

"True, I did not, but I did find the name Welton, and the receptionist and porters could easily pick you out of an identity parade. Moreover you are a very poor conspirator, sir, for you gave a false name but the correct address."

"Ah! That was a mistake," said Mowbray, with a sheepish grin.

"This is no laughing matter, sir," said Lestrade. "Now, you admit you were at the hotel on the night of the murder, and using an alias to boot?"

"Not much use continuing to deny it, is there? Yes, I was there."

"And you were there to meet Lomax, or Williams, as he was calling himself?"

Mowbray hesitated. "Well ... yes, if you press the point."

Lestrade said, "We know that Lomax was a blackmailer, sir. Was he blackmailing you?"

Again Mowbray hesitated, then, "As a matter of fact he was, or he was trying to."

"Over share deals done five or six years go?" asked Holmes.

Mowbray nodded. "That's right. He'd got hold of some old contract notes ... very similar to those you have there, as a matter of fact ... oh, all quite innocent and capable of being explained, but also capable of being misinterpreted by anyone prejudiced against me."

"He offered to sell you them?"

"Yes. He didn't have the originals, but he had copies, which he gave me to study, as he put it. I duly studied them, and concluded that, although they were capable of being misconstrued as meaning that some clients might have had cause for complaint, there was nothing in them that would prove ... conclusively prove before a judge and jury ... anything. So I told him to ... well, you can guess."

"And how did he take that?" asked Holmes.

"To tell you the truth, he seemed a bit nonplussed. I don't think he was expecting that response," said Mowbray, smiling. "But I ..." he broke off, and shrugged. "I might as well tell you. It occurred to me that it would be ... safer, less ambiguous, as it were, if the papers were in my possession. Mud sticks, you know, and the notes were capable of misinterpretation, it's a fact. So I offered him terms. In the end he settled for my buying him a steamer ticket to the Continent, for next week." He nodded to a writing desk that stood in a corner. "I still have it, as a matter of fact, if you'd care to see it for yourselves?"

Holmes shook his head. "I'm sure you have. What happened to the copies of the notes which he gave you?"

"I'll bet you burned them!" I put in.

"As a matter of fact, Doctor, I did."

"I knew it. No other course open to you."

Holmes asked, "And what of the originals?"

Mowbray shrugged. "You tell me, sir. I assumed that he did not have them upon his person, or why should he bother with copies? Hidden away at his lodgings, perhaps, or at his bank?"

"And you wouldn't be too bothered if I were to unearth them, despite your having chaffered with Lomax for their return?" asked Lestrade.

"Well, since the documents are not germane to any of your investigations, they would probably not be made public anyway," said Mowbray carefully. "Or at any rate I should hope they would not. True, if they were circulated there might be some temporary unpleasantness, but that's all. No, Inspector, I have nothing to fear from your inquiries."

"H'mm." Lestrade stood up and offered his hand. "Well, sir, it would have been better had you come forward when you read of the murder, or if you had told us the truth just now at the outset. And I must warn you that if evidence of any wrongdoing on your part does come to light, I'll be back with some questions that won't be laughed off so easily."

We set off for the street, but I paused on the threshold. "Carry on, Lestrade, Holmes. I'll only be a moment." I turned to Mowbray, a touch embarrassed.

"Dr. Watson?"

"Well, the fact is … when all this blows over, my own paltry investments could use a bit of an overhaul. I wondered …"

"Of course!" and he handed me his business card. "See me at any time, sir."

*****

"Well, gents," said Lestrade, "what do you think to Mr. Mowbray … 'as a matter of fact', then?"

Holmes smiled. "He was obviously bothered by your questions, Lestrade, and equally obviously relieved to be rid if us. But he had a ready explanation, and without further hard evidence … well!"

"Dr. Watson?"

"I'm not sure just what to make of Mr. Mowbray," I said. "He's pretty obviously shrewd and sharp, exactly as Mr. Silverton told us he was."

"Too shrewd, and too sharp, though?" asked Holmes with a smile.

"Now, that's just what I'm not sure about," I said. "There is a fine line between sharp intellect and sharp practice. If the clients have no reason to complain, and since Mowbray has kept his nose clean recently … and that on the testimony of Mr. Silverton, who was trying to put his employer in the worst possible light ... then there is probably no reason to suspect Mowbray."

"H'mm," said Holmes.

"You disagree, though?" I asked him.

"Not insofar as the possible embezzlement goes. But there is another, more serious, matter, and that is the convenient death of the senior partner."

"I thought Mowbray explained that, though?"

"Oh, to be sure," said Holmes with a laugh. "He had a glib explanation for everything, did he not? But there are ways of killing a man other than dosing him with enough arsenic to persist for a couple of centuries. Suppose for a moment that Lomax had uncovered evidence which did not relate to share dealings but to murder? An entry in the poison book, a receipt for rat bait, something more subtle? Mowbray would not face a heavier penalty for killing two men than for killing one, so the thought may have occurred to him to get rid of Lomax and so prevent the earlier crime coming to light."

"By Heaven!" said Lestrade, "I've half a mind to go back and arrest him now!"

"And what about Peter Blake?"

"Ah, yes. They can't both be guilty, can they? Unless, that is, they were in it together?"

Holmes shook his head. "Let us first interview this man MacNeil, and then the matter may become somewhat clearer," he said. "Have you the order, Lestrade?"

Lestrade tapped his inside pocket. "Safe and sound, Mr. Holmes."

"Will you telegraph to Princetown to let them know we are coming?"

Lestrade considered this. "I think not," he said, "There is a better telegraph in prison than ever the General Post Office invented! If MacNeil knows we are coming, he will have time to rehearse his story. Let it come as a surprise."

"In that event, Watson and I shall meet you at the station first thing tomorrow," said Holmes, shaking the little detective's hand. "And now, Watson, let us go to Baker Street, and investigate what Mrs Hudson can produce for supper at such short notice."

*****

We met Lestrade as arranged on the following morning, and a long but pleasant journey, during which we talked of old times, brought us to the halt nearest the great convict prison at Princetown. A couple of miles in a hired carriage, and we got down before the massive gates, and Lestrade struck sharply on the wood.

A tiny window opened in the wicket gate, and a grim looking warder stared out. "What … oh, it's you, Inspector. We didn't expect you today." He swung the gate open for us.

Lestrade produced his order, and the warder glanced at it, then started. "MacNeil?" said he. "But … have you not heard?"

"Heard what?" asked Lestrade. "Not escaped, has he?"

"Not unless you count that final escape from earthly woes that the padre talks about at church parade," said the warder with a mirthless smile.

"What d'you mean, man?"

"Well, sir, there was a fracas, a fight, yesterday, in the exercise yard. In the course of that fight, someone stuck a home-made knife into MacNeil. The doctors don't expect him to live out the day!"

Ten

"It is as the warder at the gate told you, gentlemen," said the governor as he led the way to the prison hospital. "The prisoners were out in the yard, taking their exercise under the eye of the guards, all as usual. A fight broke out in one corner of the yard, and the warders moved swiftly to break it up. When they had done so, they noticed a body slumped in another corner. It was MacNeil, and he had been stabbed with a crudely fashioned knife. The cells are searched regularly, of course, but these weapons sometimes evade our scrutiny. One of the warders tested the knife for finger marks, but without success."

"Absolute nonsense!" muttered Holmes, half to himself.

The governor paused in mid-stride. "I assure you, Mr. Holmes ..."

"No, no," said Holmes, waving a hand. "I meant no criticism of your account, which I am sure is correct in every particular. I meant only that it is nonsense to suppose that it is coincidence that this man, MacNeil, should be stabbed nearly to death on the very day that Inspector Lestrade here applies for an order to interview him!"

"It would be a monstrous coincidence, I agree," said Lestrade, thoughtfully. "And yet, Mr. Holmes, a coincidence it must be, for who knew that we were going to speak to MacNeil?"

"And what of the practicalities?" I asked. "Even assuming that the knife had been made weeks, months, ago, the word would have to be passed to the prisoners to carry out the attack. And what of the other prisoners, those who fought in order to provide a diversion whilst MacNeil was stabbed? They faced extra punishment for their part in the affair, so how would their co-operation be gained?"

It was the governor, an old military man, who answered me. "You'd be surprised, Doctor. News reaches the prisoners in a marvellous way, and once inside the walls it travels like wildfire. As for securing the co-operation of these chaps, all you really need do is tell that they're helping to do down the warders, and they'll follow you anywhere. If you need to apply yet more leverage, as it were, most of them have families, wives and children. The promise of a few guineas to the family ... or the threat of harm to it ... works wonders."

"I see. But even so, to do so much at such short notice! It is quite a little military operation, is it not?"

"It certainly argues a high degree of co-ordination, of planning," said Holmes. "Contacts in high place ... and in low! But let me ask you your own question, Lestrade ... who knew that we were coming here? Who knew of your obtaining the order to see MacNeil?"

Lestrade scratched his head. "A couple of dozen men at the Yard," he said. "But nobody who's what you might call unofficial, Mr. Holmes."

"Here we are," said the governor, halting before a door. "I'll leave you gentlemen to it," and he nodded, and left us.

The prison doctor looked up as we entered the hospital wing, and greeted Lestrade, who was evidently an old acquaintance, before looking at Holmes and me. Lestrade made the introductions, then asked, "Can we see MacNeil?"

"Oh, you can see him. But that's about all you will do," and he shared some medical details with me, at the end of which Holmes looked a question, and I shook my head.

"But can he talk?" asked Holmes.

"After a fashion," said the doctor. "But he's rambling a good deal, poor devil, and his language is not always of the purest. Still, you're all men of the world, you'll see how it is with him," and he led us to a bed upon which lay the form, much bandaged, of a middle-aged man.

"MacNeil?" said Lestrade.

"Who's that?" asked MacNeil. I make no attempt to reproduce in print the pauses and gasps which punctuated his speech; as you have gathered, the poor devil was only too clearly dying, and every word was an effort.

"Inspector Lestrade, from Scotland Yard."

"Lestrade? Don't know you, sir. Come to catch the so-and-sos who've done for me, have you?"

"I'll look into it," said Lestrade. "See here, MacNeil, it was about another matter that we came here. Forgery. Your forgery, in fact."

"Did a proper job, didn't I, sir? Even you would have to say as much. Good as the Mint. These youngsters, now ... no pride in the job, the so-and-sos."

"Just so. Now, MacNeil, you remember when you were arrested?"

"Arrested? Yes, but it wasn't you, Inspector. Let me see, now ... Haslet, was that it? Yes, Inspector Haslet."

"Haslet, that's right," said Lestrade. "Now, he took your dies, for the fake sovereigns, didn't he?"

"He did, the something so-and-so! And even he had to admire them, proper job I did, and no mistake. And the judge ... 'best fakes I've seen', and him all in his robes, too. Here, have you seen Letty?"

Holmes looked at Lestrade, who shrugged. "His lady friend, I imagine." To MacNeil, he said, "Yes, Letty's fine. She sends her love, and asks you to answer our questions. Now, Inspector Haslet took the dies, but what about the plate?"

"Plate?"

"Yes, the plate for the forged five pound notes?"

"Yes, that was funny, wasn't it?" said MacNeil with an obvious effort.

"What was funny?" asked Lestrade.

"No plate."

"What, there was no plate?"

"There wasn't no plate. Never no plate. Funny, that," and MacNeil turned away and muttered incoherently.

The doctor said, "That's about the most he's said since he came in here. But I don't think you'll get much more out of him." He bent over MacNeil, then straightened up, his face grim. "Indeed, nobody will get any more out of the poor devil."

We said our farewells to the governor, and set off back to the station. Lestrade said, "Bit of a waste of time, that, wasn't it? Pity about MacNeil, of course."

"You think our time was wasted, then?" asked Holmes.

"You heard him yourself, sir," said Lestrade. "He told us that there was no plate."

"Ah, but he also said that it was funny that there was no plate."

Lestrade frowned. "Meaning ... meaning that there should have been one, sir?"

Holmes nodded. "This inspector who handled the case ... Haslet?"

"No, Mr. Holmes, you're wrong there," said Lestrade. "Why, Superintendent Haslet's a good pal of mine."

"So good a pal, in fact, that you told him about the order to see MacNeil?"

"Why ... yes! What with it being him who originally arrested MacNeil and so on."

"I think a short talk with Superintendent Haslet is indicated," said Holmes.

*****

Superintendent Haslet was a man approaching retirement. He had a florid face, and a merry eye, and he waved us to chairs. "Well, Lestrade? You look very serious. And you, Mr. Holmes ... on a case, are you?"

Lestrade answered him. "It's a delicate matter, Superintendent," he said. "Concerning a man called MacNeil, a forger."

"Oh! Now, you're the second man who's mentioned that old case just lately. I did hear some tale that poor MacNeil had been killed in a riot or something of the sort at the prison. That right?"

"It's right enough, sir," said Lestrade. "And it was about the original arrest that I wished to speak to you, if you don't mind."

"Why should I mind? Though it is several years ago, and my memory may be a trifle hazy. That said, fire away, Inspector."

"You yourself arrested MacNeil, is that so?"

Haslet nodded. "I was just an inspector myself, then. The Treasury people were interested, of course, and when we got the tip that MacNeil was making the dud coins, we raided the place."

"One moment," said Holmes, "you say that Treasury officials were concerned?"

"Oh, yes. Natural, of course. Chap named Winterton, an acquaintance of mine, as a matter of fact, though he wasn't at the time. We met during the discussions relating to the case, you see."

"Winterton? And this man Winterton, was he with you when you raided MacNeil's premises?"

Haslet nodded. "We ... the Yard, I mean ... made the actual arrests, then Winterton more or less took over, confiscated the dies, and what have you. We eventually took custody of them, for the trial, though by that time the Treasury had defaced them. For obvious reasons," he added with a smile.

"Indeed. Tell me," said Holmes, "have you by any chance spoken to this Mr. Winterton lately?"

"Why, yes. He was he man who was asking about MacNeil. You know him, though," said Haslet.

"I? No, I don't think I've met him."

"You have! Why, he was involved in this latest murder of yours. He was acting for the Treasury, though he may have used a false name, as these chaps do."

"Yes," said Holmes, nodding, "he used the name ..."

"Dennison!" cried Lestrade and I together.

"Of course it was Dennison," said Holmes. "I suspected it from the very outset."

"Oh, yes?" said Lestrade sceptically.

"Oh, but I did. Was it not Watson here who made the point that, had the gang intercepted the note, they would have destroyed it? There were but two possibilities, that Miss Blake had revealed the note's contents to her brother, or that Dennison was acting on his own. We naturally suspected Miss Blake, but we were wrong."

"Well, but it was a monstrous coincidence her brother being there!" said Lestrade.

"Ah, but the alternative was even more monstrous, for it would require that Miss Blake knew of her brother's involvement in the forgeries, and had managed to secure employment in the investigation branch of the Treasury to help him! Dennison found the forged plate when he and the Superintendent here raided MacNeil's premises. Dennison kept the plate, with a view to going into business on his own account. And who better? After all, he told us that he had written monographs on the fine art of forgery!"

"But if this theory is correct, Holmes, then Dennison has had the plate for eight years or so," I said. "Why has he waited so long to go into business, then?"

Holmes shrugged. "Perhaps he is nearing retirement, and looks forward to a little luxury? Or perhaps it was the paper which defeated him for so long ... we dismissed the theory that the paper was genuine, stolen from the Treasury, but who knows? Perhaps Dennison has been sneaking out a few sheets at a time, claiming they were spoiled in the printing, or something of that sort? Or perhaps he just had not found a paper maker who could produce the correct quality? There are plenty of possibilities."

"That's true," said Lestrade. He started to get up. "Well, gents, I can see that we'll have to have a little chat with Mr. Dennison."

"One moment, Lestrade," said Holmes. "Your zeal does you credit, as always, but there may be an advantage in waiting."

"And let him get away?"

"And if you arrest him? You may have difficulty proving your case, I think."

Lestrade sat down again. "Forgery and murder, Mr. Holmes?"

"Proof?"

"I could always ask to borrow his penknife!" said Lestrade with a grin.

Holmes waved an impatient hand. "The fact that a man does not have a penknife does not ..."

"Only joking, sir." Lestrade scratched his head, as an aid to thought. "H'mm, I see the difficulty. If Dennison is our man, he won't have the forged plate on him, or at his house."

"And moreover, Dennison is pretty clearly not the only member of the gang," Holmes pointed out. "The fact that he was able to meet Lomax ... in his true, if such is the right word, guise as a Treasury agent ... means that Lomax could not have known that Dennison was connected with the gang. That implies a large organization, and one in which those at the bottom of the hierarchy do not know the identity of those at the top. You could arrest Dennison, to be sure. You might even make the charges stick, though frankly I doubt it. But the lesser fry would escape, along with the plate, and such forged notes as are still uncirculated."

"What would you do, then?" asked Lestrade.

"It requires the co-operation of Superintendent Haslet," said Holmes.

The Superintendent sat up straight. "Just name it, Mr. Holmes. This villain had fooled me, and I would wish, if I could, to see him get what's coming to him!"

"It is nothing too demanding," said Holmes. "Merely that, when next you see him, you mention that Lestrade here went to see MacNeil, and gained some valuable clues."

Haslet frowned. "I can go round to see him at any time, for I promised to keep him up to date with the case," he said.

"But he will already know that MacNeil died without saying much."

"Ah, but he was not there himself, so he does not know just what MacNeil may have said, or how coherent the poor fellow may have been. No, say that MacNeil, with his expert knowledge of forgery and of forgers, was able to give the Inspector here a clue, a pointer to another man, here in London. And say that the Inspector is even now waiting only for a warrant to go and search the premises of this fictitious man. Can you do that?"

"Flush him out, that it? I'll do it now," said Haslet, standing up.

*****

Inspector Lestrade nudged me in the ribs, and pointed out of the window of the cab towards the imposing portals of Her Majesty's Treasury. "There he is," he announced. "He's leaving work early, even if he isn't our man! Just keep down out of sight, Mr. Holmes, if you will, we don't want him to spot us yet."

Holmes ignored this slur, and asked, "Have you enough men, Inspector?"

"The two cabs at the end of the road are ours, sir. We don't know how many there are in the gang … or how desperate they will be. Ah, he's getting a cab, is he? Well, our driver is one of my men, and he'll keep up with him, be assured."

Off went the cab with Dennison – as I shall continue to call him – in it, and we duly followed, out of the city and across the river, into a district that was none too salubrious. "I hope your man knows his business," said Holmes, "for a cab here seems a trifle out of place."

"He knows his business, sir," said Lestrade. "And if he doesn't, I'll know the reason why!"

But the driver did know his business, and we were a hundred yards behind Dennison's cab as it drew up at a large and dilapidated warehouse. Dennison himself got down and tapped on a shabby wooden door, which was opened a moment later by someone whose face we could not see. Dennison spoke briefly, and they both went inside, closing the door after them.

Lestrade told the driver to stop. "I don't know if there's another way out," he told us, gazing at the blank wall before him. "Oh, yes, there's a fire escape. Here, you," he told one of the constables who had joined us, "stay here and watch those steps, will you? The rest of you, follow me," and he put his shoulder to the door.

As we burst into the dark and untidy room, three men, Dennison and two others, turned round in amazement. The two unknown men grasped the situation quicker than Dennison did, and attempted to flee, but we had surprise on our side, and they were quickly apprehended.

Dennison himself did not try to run, but simply stood there, astonishment – and guilt, if ever I saw it – written large on his face. "Inspector?" he managed at last, "what is the meaning of this?"

"May I ask what you're doing here, sir, so far from the office?"

"No, you my not. I am under no obligation to explain myself ... Mr. Holmes, please keep away from that cupboard! It is none of your business, sir!"

"Perhaps not, but it is certainly Inspector Lestrade's business," said Holmes, taking out a little Morocco leather case, and opening it. "H'mm, you have looked after it carefully, I see. A pity that it will have to be officially destroyed, for it is, in its own way, a work of art."

Lestrade took the case, and lifted out a metal plate. "Almost as good as the Mint, just as poor MacNeil boasted," he said. "Thank you, Mr. Holmes, it's time for the regular forces to take over now."

Eleven

"We are going well," said Holmes, looking out of the railway carriage window and glancing at his watch. "Around fifty-one and three-quarter miles per hour."

"You can"t possibly have worked that out!" I complained.

Holmes laughed. "Well, I had a talk with the driver before we left," he said.

"Speaking of going, what makes a man like Dennison go wrong, d'you think?"

Holmes shrugged. "The usual. Greed, a double life? Who can say? Perhaps it will come out at the trial."

"And then, what if Peter Blake had not been so conveniently there to take the blame for killing Lomax?"

"Oh, in that event Dennison would simply say that some other ... unknown ... member of the gang had killed Lomax. All very sad, but what could Dennison do to prevent it?"

"Yes, I see." I looked out of the window. "We are going well. I look forward to resuming our holiday."

"Indeed. Let us hope there are no more unexpected events, eh, Watson?"

"Let us hope so. Though one can never guarantee an uneventful time with you, Holmes!"

"With five volumes you could fill that gap on that second shelf."
(Sherlock Holmes, *The Empty House*)

So why not complete your collection of murder mysteries from Baker Street Studios? Available from all good bookshops, or direct from the publisher. To see full details of all our publications, range of audio books, and special offers visit www.crime4u.com where you can also join our mailing list.

MYSTERY OF A HANSOM CAB
SHERLOCK HOLMES AND DR. CRIPPEN
SHERLOCK HOLMES AND THE ABBEY SCHOOL MYSTERY
SHERLOCK HOLMES AND THE ADLER PAPERS
SHERLOCK HOLMES AND THE BAKER STREET DOZEN
SHERLOCK HOLMES AND THE BOLSHEVIK PLOT
SHERLOCK HOLMES AND THE BOULEVARD ASSASSIN
SHERLOCK HOLMES AND THE CASE OF THE HISSING SHAFT
SHERLOCK HOLMES AND THE CHARLIE CHAPLIN AFFAIR
SHERLOCK HOLMES AND THE CHILFORD RIPPER
SHERLOCK HOLMES AND THE CHINESE JUNK AFFAIR
SHERLOCK HOLMES AND THE CIRCUS OF FEAR
SHERLOCK HOLMES AND THE DISAPPEARING PRINCE
SHERLOCK HOLMES AND THE DISGRACED INSPECTOR
SHERLOCK HOLMES AND THE EGYPTIAN HALL ADVENTURE
SHERLOCK HOLMES AND THE FRIGHTENED GOLFER
SHERLOCK HOLMES AND THE GIANT'S HAND
SHERLOCK HOLMES AND THE GREYFRIARS SCHOOL MYSTERY
SHERLOCK HOLMES AND THE HAMMERFORD WILL
SHERLOCK HOLMES AND THE HILLDROP CRESCENT MYSTERY
SHERLOCK HOLMES AND THE HOLBORN EMPORIUM
SHERLOCK HOLMES AND THE HOUDINI BIRTHRIGHT
SHERLOCK HOLMES AND THE LONG ACRE VAMPIRE
SHERLOCK HOLMES AND THE MAN WHO LOST HIMSELF
SHERLOCK HOLMES AND THE MORPHINE GAMBIT
SHERLOCK HOLMES AND THE SANDRINGHAM HOUSE MYSTERY
SHERLOCK HOLMES AND THE SECRET MISSION
SHERLOCK HOLMES AND THE SECRET SEVEN
SHERLOCK HOLMES AND THE TANDRIDGE HALL MYSTERY
SHERLOCK HOLMES AND THE TELEPHONE MURDER MYSTERY
SHERLOCK HOLMES AND THE THEATRE OF DEATH
SHERLOCK HOLMES AND THE THREE POISONED PAWNS
SHERLOCK HOLMES AND THE TITANIC TRAGEDY
SHERLOCK HOLMES AND THE TOMB OF TERROR
SHERLOCK HOLMES AND THE YULE-TIDE MYSTERY
SHERLOCK HOLMES: A DUEL WITH THE DEVIL
SHERLOCK HOLMES AT THE RAFFLES HOTEL
SHERLOCK HOLMES AT THE VARIETIES
SHERLOCK HOLMES ON THE WESTERN FRONT
SHERLOCK HOLMES: THE GHOST OF BAKER STREET
SPECIAL COMMISSION
THE ADVENTURE OF THE SPANISH DRUMS
THE CASE OF THE MISSING STRADIVARIUS
THE ELEMENTARY CASES OF SHERLOCK HOLMES
THE TORMENT OF SHERLOCK HOLMES
THE TRAVELS OF SHERLOCK HOLMES
WATSON'S LAST CASE

Baker Street Studios Limited, Endeavour House, 170 Woodland Road, Sawston, Cambridge CB22 3DX

www.ingramcontent.com/pod-product-compliance
Lightning Source LLC
Chambersburg PA
CBHW042145170626
46815CB00006BA/310